REINDEER

GARETH BARSBY

REINDEER

First Edition
Gareth Barsby, Author
Sarah E. Glenn, Editor
Darby Campbell, Associate Editor
Cover by Gareth Barsby and Gwen Mayo
Copyright © 2016 Gareth Barsby
Published by Mystery and Horror, LLC
Tarpon Springs, FL

DEDICATION

Dedicated to the memory of my father, Paul Martin Barsby.

Chapter 1

The time has come.

Halloween was all over and done with, and Randall had spent all day ignoring it. No trick or treaters came to his flat, he forgot his usual pub crawl for his recliner felt much more enticing, and he didn't even watch any horror movies. No, November the first was the herald of a two month long ritual. A gradual cleansing of the rest of the years' worries and pains. A tradition he had begun not that long ago but had waited for all year.

Christmas. Or at least preparations for it.

No, preparing for Christmas was still Christmas. Christmas didn't refer to just one day, it referred to an entire period. December 25th was just the climax, no not even that. There was Christmas Day, followed by New Years and then it all ended on January 6th. And why just limit it to three weeks?

Decorations went up today. Just one or two; just something to remind him of the season.

Since he had a tendency to drop off at work or run on autopilot, Randall had begun a series of rituals in the morning to keep him awake. An extra cup of coffee, maybe an herbal energy pill. Doing the puzzle page in the Daily Mail, the only thing that paper was good for. Putting up a decoration every morning and thinking about it — what it represents, where it'd look best — would help awake his brain, ready for the computers and offices.

So up went the single strand of tinsel. What was it about tinsel that evoked Christmas? Because a lot of tinsel is red like Santa and green like Christmas trees. Or; alternatively, it was because it was sparkly like the star that led the Wise Men to Jesus. Of course, that element of the season couldn't be overlooked, concerns about political correctness aside.

So where was this tinsel going to go? Randall decided it shouldn't be anywhere too public. So many of his friends had complained about the Christmas music and the Christmas decorations and the Christmas DVDs being in the shops since September, so imagine if Rob or Dick came over and saw a big line of tinsel dangling right in front of them.

Over the bed then. His bed was the most private place in the entire flat, especially since he and Alice had gone their separate ways. So up went the tinsel, giving the unmade duvet an air of simple regality. A bed fit for a king. Then he had the mental image of Henry VIII having tinsel over his bed 365 days a year and the laugh he had actually woke him up. And he hadn't even had his coffee.

Randall lay down on his bed, and let his gaze wander around the room. The tinsel was needed; the walls looked far too placid and colourless without it. The thought of placid things reminded him that he had to get ready for work, so he sprung up towards his cupboard. He did have a Christmas tie – a purple one depicting a reindeer flying – and of course, the temptation to wear it tingled in his gut. But no, black tie. White shirt and the cleanest jacket and trousers. The grey ones. Grey meant serious and work was serious.

After taking one last look at the tinsel cellotaped over his resting place, if only to make sure it would stay put, Randall locked all the doors and entered the monochrome city. His dress shoes clacking on the pavement seemed to echo, a soundtrack that only seemed to emphasise the city's hollowness. The sky was grey, the buildings were grey, the pavement was a different shade of grey, but they all seemed to blend into each other. Randall found this appropriate, for grey was a serious colour.

He walked past a puddle, reminding him that it had rained the night before. The poor trick-or-treaters. That one shop over there still had a giant jack-o-lantern in the window, one with a big dopey grin. The one spot of colour in this otherwise washed-out street.

What am I thinking? November was for Christmas thoughts. Since Halloween was over, Randall told himself not to think about it.

Randall, sighing, stood at the bus stop along with a trio of other people. Two of them were teenagers, obviously a couple, making goo-goo eyes at each other. A wrinkled woman, seemingly unaware of the world around her, stood listening to something on headphones. She was bobbing her head and everything. Randall had never seen an old person with a MP3 player before, and wondered whether or not he should snap a picture and sell it to a newspaper.

The boyfriend and the girlfriend were wearing matching black parkas with grey trimming – probably just to be cute. Randall had a similar mindset when he was their age, doing cute things just for cuteness' sake. Still, the coats they were wearing, all thick and furry like teddy bears, meant that winter was coming. November wasn't Autumn, November was winter. September was Autumn, October was Autumn. Autumn was pumpkins and leaves and Back to School sales.

So he got on the bus with the other three, choosing a seat near the window. He had passed by those buildings so many times, and yet took them for granted, even when so many of them had such good memories for him. Not too far from here was the cinema where Randall had seen his first movie as a kid. He could still remember it so clearly, even if it had happened decades ago. Mum was out visiting a friend so it was just him and Dad, going to the theatre. It was Mum's idea, too; she wasn't much of a film buff, so she didn't mind sitting it out. Randall still remembered holding a big bag of chocolates, waiting patiently for the red curtains to part so he could eat them. *The Aristocats* was what they saw, and he was singing the songs on the ride back home.

No, this wasn't working. His mind wasn't getting more focussed, it was getting lighter. He would spend the whole work day daydreaming about childhood memories and fanciful things. No, the past and kiddie stuff and Christmas – especially Christmas, said the little voice that lived in his brain – had to be saved for the flat.

Time to think about work. Time to think about computers.

He remembered the first time he wrote a letter to Santa through e-mail.

Then he arrived at his workplace. The big office building that looked like a dull brown castle, the grass and the big blue sign outside doing little to add colour. It was not too far from the more vibrant shopping centre, which made the cloud that seemed to hover over it larger. It was a big miserable slab, looming over the road.

His mind was focussed on work and everything related to being a sales data clerk. He was thinking about computers, the office and, for the first time in years, what he learned during his maths courses in university. He entered, signed in, and sat at his usual spot in his usual squeaky chair.

In December, he would sometimes put a little Christmas tree by his computer. No-one complained, so he kept on doing it. Big thoughts about Christmas might overtake thoughts about admin, but little thoughts about it were all right.

An hour of tapping away at sales data – despite what he had planned, he went onto autopilot again and became a data entry zombie – and his mind awoke again when someone said, 'Hey!'

He looked up. Lenny, Alice's new boyfriend. The guy with the Mercedes and the money he had gotten from daddy, always with that idiotic grin framed by his beard. Oh, what to say to him...

'Hi.'

'This is your time, isn't it?' asked Lenny.

'What do you mean?'

'November and December. That's the best time to talk to you. I mean, I tried to talk with you in August, and you had your head hung over like some sort of moody teenager. Alice told me you were more yourself during this time of year.'

'Did she?'

'Yeah,' said Lenny, 'I think I've got something that may be up your street.'

'Oh, really?'

'Yeah, you know how they're always holding a Christmas Festival in town near the beginning of December?'

That event was a top priority for Randall, an essential ingredient of his annual recipe. He'd go there, have some of the snacks and even buy some of the cute little projects for himself and for his mum. They even had a Santa's Grotto for the kiddies –Randall had contemplated visiting it once or twice even.

'Well,' said Lenny, 'They're holding auditions tomorrow for volunteers.'

'Volunteers?'

'Voluntary actors,' said Lenny, striking his best "Alas, Poor Yorick" pose. 'Alice told me you used to do theatre.'

'Did she?' Yes, he had been in a drama group; they mostly did Shakespeare plays and he never really had that much of a big role in them, but it was where he met Alice in the first place. She was the one playing Ophelia while he was one of the guards who saw the ghost.

—

4

They struck up a conversation, and this led to them having a cup of coffee after the show.

'Yeah,' replied Lenny, sounding slightly upset, 'Anyway, this festival is going to have a big stage and have a bit of a variety show. There's going to be some kids singing Christmas carols, and we're going to have *The Night Before Christmas* and various scenes from *A Christmas Carol*. Yes, that would be probably the zillionth adaptation of that story, but it should still be fun.'

Randall froze in his seat at the very mention of *A Christmas Carol*, the very thing he credited to his need to do the two month long tradition. *Aristocats* wasn't the first movie he ever saw; it was *Mr. Magoo's Christmas Carol*. Dad said it was his favourite Christmas movie growing up and shared it with Randall via an old VHS tape.

'Yeah, I'll think about it,' replied Randall, as if by instinct.

'Great, talk to you later,' said Lenny as he walked off.

And Randall would talk to him later. This was the season to be jolly…wait, no big Christmas thoughts at the workplace, remember? But Lenny had mentioned *A Christmas Carol* and *A Christmas Carol* was about being good and how could Randall say he loved *A Christmas Carol* if he wasn't good? Though, did that bearded dick deserve talking to? He deserved a talking-to, that's for sure. He and Alice had been dating for three years, and then with a 'It's not working out' she runs to him as if he had her under mind control or something.

No, that's the type of attitude Scrooge might have, isn't it? And he knew from childhood that he didn't want to be Scrooge. First it was Mister Magoo, and then came the Muppets and Mickey Mouse, followed by Alistair Sim and George C Scott. Scrooge was mean and selfish, and that meant he had to be visited by three ghosts, or four rather. Marley, Past, Present and the tall black shade, the figure with the skeletal claws and the blankness where there should be a face.

Randall went back to his data entry, but of course, the image of the Ghost of Christmas Yet to Come was leering over him, shaking its hooded head and wagging its skeletal finger at him. Randall recalled a nightmare he had, one where he stood in a monochrome forest under an overcast sky and dead trees. There waited the Ghost of Christmas Yet to Come, its cloak resembling splotches of ink. It pointed to a gravestone sticking out of the grey, cracked ground. His father's grave.

Soon, however, he got a bit of free time and was able to catch up with Lenny, who arched an eyebrow as Randall arrived. 'You okay?'

'Yeah, why?'

'You're still okay with Alice, aren't you?'

'Yeah, I just want to know more about the voluntary thing, and like you said, we should just chat. We haven't really spoken to each other.' But what to talk about… 'Did you do anything for Halloween?'

'Oh, that,' said Lenny, stroking his beard as if impersonating a stereotypical wizard. 'Me and Alice went to the pub. They had free shots for anyone who went in fancy dress.' He sniggered slightly. 'I went as Mr. Toad with a big frog mask. I asked Alice if she wanted to be Ratty or Moley, but she just wanted to go as a witch, so I let her.'

Thinking of nothing better to say, Randall responded, 'Okay.'

'We had a good night,' continued Lenny, 'We didn't encounter any ghosts though,' he added, laughing at his own joke.

'Ghosts aren't real.'

'They can be,' said Lenny, smiling. 'If you volunteer, you could play one of the *Christmas Carol* ghosts. I can see you being the big fat bearded one.'

'You mean the Ghost of Christmas Present?'

'Oh yeah, him.'

'Okay,' said Randall, 'I'll give it a shot.' A second after saying that, Randall wondered why he sounded like he had been defeated. Why he wouldn't want to do this? This was supposed to be the time of year where he would have the holiday spirit, and if he were to have the holiday spirit, he should give the holiday spirit. He certainly didn't want to be the Santa in a Santa's grotto – those Santas always had cold, dead eyes, rather than the joyful sparkly ones Santa should have – but now that he had the opportunity to play characters from a book that made an impact on him, why not take it?

'Really, you OK?' asked Lenny. 'You just zoned out a bit there.'

'I'm fine,' repeated Randall. 'So, anything else been happening with you?'

Lenny then blathered on about his life from the last year, but Randall listened to very little of it. He caught bits and pieces but his mind was too swamped with work and Christmas and admin and ghosts.

He then returned to his computer, where he strangely found himself back on autopilot, and before he knew it, work was over and it was time to go home. And on Friday, no less. With all the duties of a data clerk done, now the big Christmas thoughts could come in. What Christmas decorations to put up next, what Christmas treats to eat in the coming weeks, what Christmas movies to watch, what Christmas

—

roles to play.

Auditions for volunteers were tomorrow, and he would go along to it. He knew the lines to the story by heart from having watched so many versions – and of course, having read the book- and he even had one or two things that could be used as costumes. He even had a Grim Reaper costume that he wore for Halloween.

Despite the fact that he usually took the bus home, he decided to walk it this time. He was getting chubby – it wasn't like a big bowl of jelly, though – and he could use the exercise. He didn't go straight home, though, he took a quick detour into the shopping centre. There, he saw true November. A bunch of wannabe writers huddled round discussing their novels. People wearing parkas and scarves. He turned around and saw some Christmas lights. A snowman behind a window. An angel with a carol sheet attached to the same window.

Seeing these, Randall felt he was right. He was right in what he was doing. He wasn't the only one.

Most of the shops were beginning to close, but there was one still open, or at least open long enough for Randall to get what he needed. Feeling a little peckish, he got himself a croissant – when he walked out, he wondered if he should have gotten more so he could have one for breakfast – a bottle of Coke, and a three-pack of microwaveable popcorn.

That was how he was going to ring in the new season: with a holiday movie. They were in a secret CD case, buried among the *Breaking Bad* box set and both versions of *Alfie*. Normally he would engage in entertainment tailored for adults – though he wondered if he only had DVDs of *Casablanca* and *Dr. Strangelove* to make him look smarter like Rob proudly displaying an unread copy of *Moby Dick* – but this season was for cheesy children's cartoons.

The CD case boasted movies from a variety of sources: eBay, garage and car boot sales, even actual stores. The lesser Christmas movies were at the back – he still watched them every year though, and he had considered moving *Jingle All The Way* slightly higher some days – and his favourites were at the front. There was *It's A Wonderful Life* and *Gremlins* and, yes, *A Christmas Carol*. About seven or eight versions.

And which *Carol* did Randall pick? Mr. Magoo's. Because, well, why not?

After plopping it into his DVD drive, he went into the kitchen and microwaved the popcorn. The music from the DVD menu flooded the room, and suddenly, it felt like the whole flat had been completely decorated. There were no Christmas trees or poinsettias, but there might as well have been. The living room of his parents' house was decorated to the nines when Randall had first seen this movie, and the room of his flat was thus now filled with similar invisible decorations.

With the popcorn complete, Randall hit the play button. *Boy, this hasn't aged well.* In his adulthood, having consumed more sophisticated entertainment, Randall had begun to notice the flaws in this film. The animation was terrible; people walked by bobbing up and down while being slid across the screen. The Ghost of Christmas Present came before the Ghost of Christmas Past for no reason that Randall could see.

However, he couldn't think bad things about his Dad, and since Dad loved this movie, saying bad things about this movie meant he was saying bad things about Dad. What would he think if he was here right now?

Upon hearing the opening musical number again, he felt the hand of his father on his shoulder, and heard his voice as he spoke about how he loved this cartoon so when he was a kid. How he sang along with the songs. How he felt sad when Scrooge, as a child, was left all alone. How, yes, he was scared by the Ghost of Christmas Yet to Come.

Chapter 2

Randall *was* the Ghost of Christmas Yet to Come.

As per Lenny's recommendation, he had come to the auditions, and they had picked him to play the final ghost of *A Christmas Carol*. Randall had dug out his Grim Reaper costume for the audition - he went in with black robe, "invisible" mesh all over his face and a white rope around his waist, and used body language to act. In his drama group, some had told him he would be better suited for non-verbal roles. He knew what they meant by that, but here he was.

He was supposed to do one little scene, one in between "Oh, Little Town of Bethlehem" and "We Wish You a Merry Christmas". It was simply the scene where Scrooge is shown his grave and he repents. Big long speech and everything. They had a rather nice looking graveyard backdrop too, a nice monochrome backdrop with pointed iron fences and a Gothic-looking church in the fog-shrouded distance.

Lenny was there too, of course he was. He wore a Santa hat, which seemed to make him look all the more grotesque in its smugness. The big finale to the show was an adaptation of Clement C. Moore's *The Night Before Christmas*...though Lenny insisted Randall call it by the original title of *A Visit from St. Nicholas*. Lenny had even spoken to Randall in the voice he used for Santa, one that sounded like he had a cold and had marshmallows stuck in his mouth. Lenny was actually one of two Santas to be used at the festival. One for the grotto, one for the play.

One of the movies Randall had in his collection, one of the few he didn't watch every year, was one about a young couple breaking up over Christmas, and then Santa Claus, disguised as a magical homeless man, appears and gets them back together. Randall had watched that movie ironically most of the time; he saw it as a teenager and guffawed his head off at all the "soppy bits". The first Christmas after Alice got involved with Lenny, though, he suddenly felt like a kid again.

But there was no Santa Claus. No fat man in a sleigh, no sack full of presents, no flying reindeer. If Santa were real, he would be arrested for breaking and entering, a joke Randall had seen on many e-mail forwards. Randall couldn't help but feel Santa did exist. He read that Virginia letter, he watched all the specials. Santa did exist but only as an idea, a symbol to give and do good and have Christmas spirit. You can't be good without Christmas spirit.

At the audition, Randall wanted to laugh at how silly Lenny looked in that Santa hat, but restrained himself. It wouldn't be Christmassy. They were going to be in a play together, and Randall had to tolerate it and smile and be nice to Lenny. If he laughed at Lenny or had a go at him and talked about Alice, then Alice and Santa and the Christmas ghosts would be disappointed.

He wondered if he was only being nice because of Christmas movies, but decided that other entertainment had something to do with it as well. *Breaking Bad* taught him the consequences of being bad. Don't be bad or you get half your face blown off. If Santa existed in *Breaking Bad*, he would have made Walt's cancer disappear and would have given Jesse a lump of coal for making drugs.

So Randall decided not to think about Lenny. At least not the bad things. Since this wasn't a work day, it was time for big Christmas thoughts. Lenny was Santa, the man in the grotto was Santa, everyone was Santa.

In fact, to celebrate, the first thing he did when he got back home was watch another *Christmas Carol* – a low budget cartoon one, since Muppets and Sim and Scott deserved December – and another cheesy Santa cartoon. *Mr. Whiz Saves Christmas*. The evil mutant lizard Dr. Scaly had invaded Santa's workshop and was installing mind-control devices in the toys, and the superheroic Mr. Whiz - who wore spandex and a porkpie hat for some reason – had to restore things to normalcy.

Then came the day of the festival. He grabbed his Grim Reaper costume, shoved it in his backpack, and took the next bus. He saw two of the elves from the Santa's Grotto looking around the stalls, while the stalls were being staffed by people in top hats and scarves. Those elves and those shopkeepers…they didn't belong together. A Victorian man who made candles, wearing dull grey clothes, was talking with a magical little goblin that made toys and wore candy cane tights. Of course, both of them looked like anachronisms when they were close to city buildings, and were in a place with modern songs pumping through the speakers.

'Hey!'

Alice. Her herself.

Of course she had to be here. The furry hood of her parka was over her face, but Randall could still see her blazing red hair pop out, he could still see her eyes glisten, her lips were as red as ever.

'Oh, hi!' said Randall, wearing his best smile. 'You here to see Lenny?'

'Well, yeah,' replied Alice, scoffing a bit, 'I came to see you too, you silly sausage.' When Randall didn't reply, she sighed. 'You're still not over that, are you?'

'No,' replied Randall, 'no, I am.'

'I dunno, Randall,' said Alice shaking her head, 'You get way too worked up about things sometime. Mean, heck, here you are getting worked up about bloody Christmas.'

'What?' said Randall, doing his best sitcom shrug, 'Everyone gets worked up about bloody Christmas!'

'Yeah, I guess,' said Alice, rolling her eyes, 'I mean, to tell the truth, part of the reason I'm here is because mum likes these cheesy art stuff and I thought I'd get her one as a present. You know, like you got me one of those twirly candles last year.'

'Yeah,' replied Randall, though he swore he could sense a genuine pang of contempt in her words. Or maybe contempt was too extreme a word to use. Low opinion then. She still held him in con…low opinion. She held him in low opinion. Did that phrase make any sense?

'Anyway, why are you chatting to me? Don't you have a role to prepare for?'

'Yeah.'

'Hey!' Alice cried again before Randall went off. 'You want to go with me and Lenny to the Crowned Lion after the Festival?' Randall said 'Sure,' because what else could he do?

He went to prepare for the little scene he had, putting on his

Grim Reaper garb and practicing his…movements. Of course, that was the beauty of this role: no lines. Part of him wanted to ad-lib a line or two in a silly voice just to see the response of the audience. He couldn't do that to such a sacred story, but considering what so many people had done to the story already – all those sitcoms and all those cartoons – anything he could bring to the story couldn't be any worse than what was already published and aired.

Randall decided it would be better to give his voicebox a rest until the pub.

He sat there, waiting for his moment to shine. First there was a carol, then a musical number – someone singing "So Here It Is, Merry Christmas" and then the first scene of *A Christmas Carol*. Well, not the *first* first scene, rather the bit where Scrooge meets Jacob Marley. Listening to the scene, Randall wondered if he should have auditioned for the role of Marley instead of the final spirit. All that screaming and wailing awakened a little spark of inspiration, and he thought of trying for that role in the future. He had so wanted to be Hamlet's father so long, long ago. Oh well.

More carols to let the kids have their due. Besides, it was probably the only thing in the whole show that had any acknowledgement that this was supposed to be for Jesus' birthday. More *Christmas Carol* scenes followed; the Ghost of Christmas Past and Scrooge's breakup, Bob Cratchit's dinner and then Randall's big scene.

Up came the graveyard. Though it was wintery, it had nothing to do with the happy gingerbread cottage of the musical number or the warm Victorian home of the previous Carol scene. No, this was a different world, the show had switched gears. Out with Santa, in with the Reaper.

All intentions of bringing humour to the role evaporated as Randall made his way onto the stage, slinking and sliding as if he were Dracula searching for a meal. There was Scrooge, head buried in his hands, sobbing over his predicament. 'Poor Tiny Tim,' he wailed, 'How could this happen? Spirit, are these the shadows of things that will be, or are they the shadows of things that may be only?'

Randall rose like the hairs of a frightened cat. He grew, he felt like he could reach the top of the stage. Then he pointed.

'My actions have foreshadowed certain ends,' said Scrooge – this was Scrooge, not some bloke dressed up as him – 'but if the actions change, certainly the ends must change as well.'

Randall rose again. He grew huger. He pointed again.

Scrooge was on his knees as if at an altar. And why shouldn't he be? He may not have been in the presence of a god, but certainly he was near something akin to a god. Something powerful. Randall was powerful.

There was no stage. There was no audience. There was no painted backdrop. Randall could feel the shrill graveyard chill against his neck. He could smell the decay and debris all around. He could hear the distant church bells. This wasn't a play. Those were real gravestones, those were real, cold, rusted iron fences. Though no-one living was here except Scrooge, and though there were corpses underneath their feet, the graveyard was alive. Randall could hear it breathing.

'RIP,' Scrooge read aloud, 'Ebenezer...Scrooge? No! Have I died alone and unmourned?' Randall didn't say yes. He didn't even nod. He was the embodiment of the unknown, and thus had no definite answers. 'I will love Christmas in my heart! Tell me I may wash away the writing on this stone!'

What's a better motivator than fear? You are supposed to fear God, aren't you?

The scene ended and the audience applauded.

Randall had heard applause several times before, but this applause was for his sake, he knew it. The actor playing Scrooge was too over-the-top, and his dialogue was simplified as well. Randall knew he was the shining star of that one scene, playing a character with so little time and with no dialogue. People had said Scrooge was a hard character to play, but surely the Ghost of Christmas Yet to Come must be even harder since there was so little to work with. Randall had made the character his. Despite his gut, he stood tall.

Then came more carols and the *Night Before...Visit from St. Nicholas* bit, but what did that matter? Randall felt he didn't need to see the rest of the festival. He had the Christmas spirit at least. All the decorations, all the DVDs he had, all the mince pies and Frosty Fancies didn't light him up, and yet this did. Taking on the form of the being that had terrorised him in childhood and interested him as an adult was what did the trick.

And he could be other Christmas characters, too. He could be Santa and give joy. He could be an elf; he could be focussed when he wanted to be and what he did at the show and the decorations he had put up at his flat showed that he could be creative.

When he took off the robe – for he knew there would be old

people about – and put on his winter jacket, he did not feel like himself. No, he was another Christmas character. He was Frosty the Snowman, the being who was brought to life by magic and afterwards began dancing down the snow-filled streets. There was no snow this Christmas – there hadn't been for the last couple of years – yet it still felt like there was. There was no such thing as Santa Claus or reindeer, but it felt like there was. Heck, the Santa that wasn't Lenny looked more like Santa than most grotto Santas did.

But no, he was Frosty. The children's hopes and wishes had brought him to life, and now he was going to dance with them in celebration. Happy Birthday indeed. Normally his brain was heavy, swamped with doubts and thoughts and memories but now it felt light, and he felt light too. Light as a feather…light as snow…and it is snowing even though it isn—

Splat

Everything was black.

Chapter 3

'Oh god, oh god. Is he going to be okay?'

His head was heavy again. Heavier than ever. In fact, it felt like he was sinking. He was descending into a pit.

'Randall! Randall, buddy! Come on!'

That was Lenny's voice. Oh God, he actually used the word "buddy". Randall would have slapped Lenny if he could move his arms. Or if he could see.

Suddenly he felt even number, if such a thing was possible. His mind grew all the heavier, being filled with more and more questions and doubts, even if he could see and hear nothing. He usually thought better when he could see things.

It then felt like something was escaping him. Like his very insides were being ripped out of him. Like his entrails and his bones and his muscles were pulled away, leaving only a lump of skin behind. That's all he was; an unmoving pile of flesh and a brain.

The voices came again. They weren't Alice or Lenny though.

'Your duty has been decided.'

Yes, voices. Those words were spoken by several different voices at the same time, though Randall didn't know if he actually heard them or if they were just in his head.

Then he felt snow. Actual snow, not the fancy-fairy stuff he was imagining before he ended up in this position. He could feel it between his fingers – his fatter, chubbier fingers – and even felt a small urge to scrunch it up and make a snowball. He tried to stand up in it, but one little slip and he fell to his stomach.

His body felt different. It was fatter and thinner and runtier and all sorts of things. His body was different and the wind was different. The wind always had a distinctive tinge to it at winter; it still had that tinge but it also had something else mixed in. Something that smelled like cinnamon, no, it smelled like fire. He was feeling fire and cold at the same time. Whatever it was gave him a chill and warmed him at the same time. He warmed himself for a while and then got up and opened his eyes.

Snow. Well, of course there was snow, that's what he felt in his hooves.

He looked down. Where there were once human hands, there were now hooves. Two big black clappy things attached to a thin brown furry arm. There was also a little primate thumb, which Randall wiggled about a bit before falling over on his back.

His hands had become hoof-hands, but his arms still operated like arms. His legs – which he wriggled about a bit - still operated like his human legs, even if they looked more or less the same as his arms. Hooves, only much fatter.

Oh god. Could it be?

Yes, he had a snout – he could see he had a black nose and felt slightly disappointed that it didn't glow. He rubbed his head with his hoof hands, standing on his new legs as he did so. Yup, big floppy ears. Big antlers. He looked up and saw a prong from one of them in front of his face.

Yes. He had turned into a reindeer.

Randall rubbed his body some more. He had fur. He had hooves and a tail and antlers. And here he was among a snowy place that was most likely the North Pole. He had turned into Dasher or Dancer or Donner.

Randall rubbed his temples, and attempted to convince himself that this was a lucid dream. He had read about dreams where you could control what happens, and he'd tried a couple of times to have one of them. What else would he dream about other than Christmas things? He remembered thinking of himself as a Christmas character, and here he was.

Here he was at the North Pole. Here he was at Santa's homeland, where he had wanted to visit when he was five. Yet now that he had actually arrived, he just stood still, covering his eyes.

'Hey! You!'

Alice. That sounded just like Alice.

He opened his eyes, half expecting to see Alice again …but no, it was another reindeer.

'Hey!' It sounded less like Alice when she said it a second time. This reindeer wasn't Alice. She was just another reindeer, standing on her hind legs like Randall was.

'Hello?' Randall managed to say. At least he knew he could talk in this form.

She chuckled. 'Hello! I'm Samantha! Welcome to Santa's homeland.'

Randall then said something that he felt had to be said. 'But…Santa's not real.'

'That's what they all say,' replied Samantha, the sentence sounding weird with the airy-fairy way she said it. 'Santa may not be real on Earth but he's real here in Purgatory.'

Randall felt like laughing, but the laugh seemed to evaporate as soon as it appeared.

'I'm sorry,' replied Samantha, though she still sounded happy, 'You're dead.'

Upon hearing that, Randall felt like fainting, but he kept upright, for at the same time, the phrase 'That makes sense' repeated through his head. If he was dead, then that "Splat", for lack of a better word, made sense. If he was dead, the blackness made sense. If he was dead, even being in Santa's workshop made sense because well, what would be a better heaven for him?

But he wasn't in Heaven, Samantha said. He was in Purgatory. Santa lived in Purgatory.

'I know you're confused,' said Samantha calmly. 'I was just like you when I first came here, but you won't believe how quickly it took for me to get adjusted here. I mean, they say I should be ascending any day now.'

'Ascending?' Randall knew what it meant, but he had to ask, just to make sure.

'Everyone in Purgatory is given a duty to do,' explained Samantha, twirling her hoof-hand. 'If they do a good job…' She stopped and looked up.

'And…my duty is to be a reindeer.' Randall stroked his body again. Yup; fur, antlers, big ears. Still a reindeer, all right.

'You died in December,' said Samantha, as she began to walk

away, and beckoned Randall to follow her. 'And you had a great love of Christmas, too. I was the same when I was a human. I had Christmas songs on my iPod in July. Helped me get through my nine-to-five, it did.' She chuckled. 'You know, if you like that sort of thing, this is the place for you.'

Samantha was walking on her hind legs, so Randall did so as well, though he did have the slight temptation to walk on all fours. If he was going to be an animal, why not act like one? After all, he was walking around in the snow completely naked and it felt no different than when he went out wearing all his clothes. Maybe now he could even poo wherever he felt like it as well.

There it was. Almost exactly how Randall had pictured it. A gigantic gingerbread cottage framed by candy canes clawing towards the purple sky. Several smaller cottages around it, each with a cute little chimney and lights illuminating the door. It looked exactly like a poster Randall had used to decorate his flat with.

All around the large cottage were other reindeer. They all stood on fours at first, then they moved to their hind legs so they could wave their arms at Randall. Randall had heard about Santa having eight tiny reindeer, but there were eight reindeer waving, and then there was Samantha and there was Randall.

'Hey!' cried Randall, turning to Samantha, 'If we're…if reindeer are supposed to be dead humans…is everyone here dead? Even the elves?'

'Yes,' said Samantha, 'This is Purgatory, after all. The elves are dead, just like us. I guess they thought you'd be a better reindeer than you would an elf.'

'Who are they?'

'I would like to tell you,' said Samantha, 'but I can't.'

Randall buried his face in one of his hoof-hands and walked away. He closed his eyes tightly, hoping to find himself back in bed. He hoped to see Mum and Alice and even Lenny. Scrunching his face, he began to think of his flat with its lonely bed and its decorations and its DVDs…

He was still naked in the snow. He still felt the warm chill. He was still in Purgatory, still a reindeer.

So he was dead. He ran out into the road and got hit and now he was in Purgatory. No more yearly two-month traditions. No more flat. He would never see his Mum or Alice again. He would never even be human again.

'C'mon, lazy!' Samantha prodded Randall until Randall opened his eyes again. 'I haven't even started the tour yet and you're already lounging about!'

'Sorry,' replied Randall, shaking his head a bit. 'Say, if this is Purgatory, have you ever met...'

Samantha raised an eyebrow – yes, she actually seemed to have eyebrows. 'Have I ever met who?'

'Never mind.'

They both entered the main cottage. After walking down a hall with tinsel and miniature Christmas trees, they came to the main workshop. Sure enough, the support beams were candy canes, and the walls were all a light green. There were long wooden tables, and the elves were all working at them. No, they weren't elves, not in the traditional sense. They were elves like the people working at Santa's Grotto were elves. They all wore the traditional grab. Robin Hood hats and tops, and the striped tights with the curly boots. No pointed ears though. No curled noses or rosy cheeks. A few of them were short, but there were regular-sized elves, and Randall turned around and saw one muscular elf. He had to hold in laughter when he saw the bulky fellow with the little pointed hat on his head.

They were making toys – some of them were, at least. He saw a couple of teddy bears being sewn up, but he also saw picture frames, photos and canvases. He also saw guitars and even an accordion.

'We make toys, yes,' said Samantha, 'but we make other things too. Things that remind the people of Purgatory of their human lives and why they are here. Just think, one of these could be the little extra push someone needs to ascend.' Her smile grew wider. 'We get presents too. If we don't ascend or descend, we get a little reward. Speaking of which...'

'Hey, Samantha,' said the muscular elf, waving. 'That the new guy?'

'Yes,' replied Samantha, and Randall felt he had no choice but to wave as well. After that, all the other elves waved, their smiles stretching their faces enough to make them look like anthropomorphic plates.

Samantha then led Randall up a flight of stairs — Randall had to duck due to how big his antlers were – and she brought him to a room with a giant screen...was that what Randall thought it was? The repetitive music, the eye-blinding colours...*Mr. Whiz Saves Christmas*. They had that! There was Dr. Scaly, singing to himself. 'We wish you an evil Christmas,' sang Dr. Scaly in that high-pitched voice of his, and as childish as it was, Randall couldn't help but guffaw at it.

'I'm glad you like it,' said Samantha, 'this is our entertainment centre. We have just about every Christmas special known to man, which, well, people like us just love. It's also a good motivator.'

'I see.' The more Randall stayed here, the easier it was for him to talk. 'Do you have *Mr. Magoo's Christmas Carol?*'

Samantha froze. Her smile instantly vanished.

'Hello?'

'OK,' said Samantha, her smile slowly returning, 'I know you're new here, but we don't really like to talk about *A Christmas Carol* here. We have every Christmas special, except those inspired by that book.'

'Why?'

'Santa thinks it lowers morale. I mean, do you really want to watch a Christmas special about dark spirits and death?'

'Well, you said we are d-'

'Sometimes Santa wants us to forget that.' Samantha looked up, drawing Randall's attention to more of those candy cane support beams. 'This land was built from dreams, not nightmares. Its very foundation was children hoping for someone to come and deliver Christmas cheer. You and I even contributed a bit, I'm sure.'

Randall didn't respond, but instead focussed on the beam. He tried to picture wishing so hard something would appear, like the Green Lantern made things appear with his magic ring. His dreams of a candy-coloured house were the same dreams millions of children had, so they all came together and created a physical place. He had cement and mortar and bricks in his head and had built Santa's workshop. Randall was reminded of those Facebook games where you bugged your friends to give you fictional supplies to help build a little house for your virtual village.

'Would you like me to take you to Santa now?' Samantha pulled Randall's face towards hers. 'He's always eager to meet new recruits.'

Meeting Santa was his dream all throughout childhood, and he even felt it time from time in adulthood. It was why he tried to sneak down into the living room at midnight, why he always liked to peek through the crack his bedroom door had. One year, he had even put chewing gum into the fireplace so Santa would get stuck and he'd have more time to catch him.

Now that he actually was about to meet Santa in the flesh, as it were, Randall felt like his stomach was turning inside out.

As Samantha took him up another staircase – with Randall having to duck again – he tried to hum to himself to soothe the crackling and bubbling in his stomach. Santa was jolly and happy and – Santa knows everything Santa will judge you Santa is...

Knock knock knock. Samantha politely knocked on an office door. 'Come in.' It didn't sound that much different from the marshmallow voice Lenny used, nor did it sound all that different from the shopping centre Santas Randall had seen through his life. Nonetheless, Randall steeled himself when he opened the door, half-expecting a shining being or Cthulhu only to find that, like everything else here, Santa was exactly how he had imagined him.

Santa was a fat balding man with a big cotton wool beard and eyebrows like that of an owl, displaying both youth and age with a shining, unwrinkled face. He wore a red jumper adorned with Randall's new species, with the collar of a yellow shirt poking out. 'Pleased to meet you, Randall,' said Santa, making Randall jump back a bit. 'Come now, you know that I know you. You've known since childhood.' Tapping his head, Santa added, 'You do have dreams, don't you?'

'Well...'

'Dreams are what brought you here. You had a bit of a daydream and went out onto the road.' Santa gestured towards the TV in his office. It went on by itself and Randall saw his human self, looking dopey, getting hit by a lorry. It looked like some sort of comedy sketch, the type of thing you'd see on a sketch show.

'But do not blame dreams for your demise,' said Santa, his fluffy voice becoming slightly more grave. 'It was after you played the Ghost of Christmas Yet to Come, wasn't it? Maybe sh...it had something to do with it.'

'What do you mean?'

'They also exist, you know, the Ghosts of Christmas, as they are called, ruining such an innocent holiday. They think they are doing good with their hauntings, but the change anyone undergoes after being haunted by them is not genuine. They believe they can make someone change by fear alone, and a change caused by fear of retribution is not a genuine change.'

He turned to Samantha, clasping his fingers together. 'Samantha here didn't need to be terrified to become our very best reindeer, did you, Samantha?'

Samantha seemed to blush. 'Thank you, Santa.'

'I'm sure you will be just as good though,' said Santa, his

marshmallow voice metamorphosing into more of a grandpa tone. 'You are to help us spread joy and happiness around Purgatory, which will help many ascend.' Randall thought he had been desensitised to saccharine through all the movies he had watched, but what he just heard made him want to vomit, Santa or not.

'Okay,' said Randall. 'How do I ascend?'

'Simply do a good job helping me deliver presents. They will decide if you are worthy.'

There was that Them again. Randall simply kept quiet.

'You will have duties to do other than pull my sleigh,' said Santa, his voice regaining some of that marshmallow-ness. 'But as this is your first day here, you may do what you wish at the moment. You may use the entertainment centre, or you may even pay a visit to Toyland.'

'Toyland?'

'Did not Samantha tell you, this is a place built by children's dreams? Though I have my elves, Toyland is also a fine supplier of gifts. Certainly you must have seen the play it inspired.' Randall remembered he had indeed: *Babes in Toyland*. The Laurel and Hardy version was one of the DVDs he saved until December. The evil Barnaby wants to marry Mary Quite Contrary and he needs to be thwarted before he ruins Toyland with his goblin army…his demons.

'You seem quite anxious, my boy,' said Santa, his eyes having that twinkle they were supposed to have. 'Randall, I will see to it that you ascend as soon as possible. You will go to Heaven, and I will even make sure your friends and family will join you if I have to. Until then, however, you may use today to get better acquainted with my home. Samantha will show you to where you will be sleeping.'

Samantha led Randall to one of those little cottages outside the big one; his own personal one. Despite looking like it could only accommodate a more traditional elf, the inside was actually fairly roomy. There was a bed, a little kitchen, a sitting area, a bookcase and even an actual toilet. Randall didn't know whether to feel relief or disappointment that he wasn't going to live in a stable like an actual animal. Living like a human had its perks, he knew, but he thought that if he were to be an animal, it would be interesting to live like one. It would have made a nice change at least.

'There you go,' said Samantha, looking like a mother sending her child off to his first day at school. 'Is there anything I can get you?'

'No,' replied Randall, 'I'm fine. I'd rather stay here, if that's all right with you.'

'Of course,' said Samantha, bowing. 'I'll see you tomorrow.'

She left, and finally Randall was alone. If he was going to be stuck in a weird land out of a children's story, he was going to need some solitude from time to time, if only to help him comprehend where he had gotten himself into. Though he had only been on his feet for about an hour or so, he felt like he needed a lie down.

The pillow on the bed was longer than usual, and fluffier too. A pillow for a reindeer with big antlers. They thought of everything here. *By "they"*, thought Randall, *I mean the people here, not the other ones people keep talking about*. Or maybe that same "they" built this place to be used by the dead. Santa could be one of Them, even. Though would members of the Them refer to themselves by that term? They never thought up a team name, maybe even an amusing acronym? Or perhaps "they" was an acronym?

Terrible Heavenly Entities of Years? They Hear Everything, Yes?

Whatever they were – and Randall was actually pretty sure he knew what they were – they had turned him into Santa's reindeer. Now he was here, he was going to have to help around the workshop, and pull Santa's sleigh across the full moon...

He slapped his head at how he could have forgotten that.

He could fly now!

There was an actual childhood fantasy he could stand to have as an adult; being able to fly. And without wings or a towel for a cape either. He burst out of his tiny little cottage, raising his arms so his naked body could embrace the freezing winds of Purgatory. He took one stride in the snow, then another, and looked upwards. Up at the purple sky, with its slivers of grey clouds and the dots of snow descending – bad choice of words there – down. He stretched his body, with it feeling comfortable for the first time since he got here and he leapt.

Then he fell face first onto the snow.

He closed his eyes yet again, expecting to hear laughter and jeers from his fellow reindeer, but instead, he felt another hoof-hand hold onto his, helping him up. Samantha again.

'Oh,' she said, 'this happens with all new recruits. You can't fly until Christmas Eve comes round, I'm afraid.'

'Why not?'

'Because Christmas Eve is when the spirit world is at its most powerful. That and Halloween, though, of course, that holiday has no place here.'

'Okay,' replied Randall, 'whatever you say.' And he returned back to his little cottage.

Chapter 4

The rest of Randall's first day was spent in his little hovel, lying on the bed, thumbing through some of the books in his bookshelf. They didn't have much variety; there was *A Visit from St. Nicholas*, of course, a kids' book of Santa stories, a book of fairy tales, a book retelling Disney's *Dumbo* – why were grim reapers not allowed here, but scary pink elephants were? – and some colouring/activity books, some Christmassy, some not. So Randall knew that Christmas stories weren't the only media consumed here, though he knew he wasn't going to see *Breaking Bad* or *Dexter* aired here any time soon.

The bed he had was more comfortable then he had expected it to be and his sleep went undisturbed. When he awoke the next morning, he checked his body again, just to see if he still had hooves, big ears and antlers. No, it still wasn't a dream. It can't be. He could feel the small fur between his hooves, the chill that was warm was unlike anything Randall had ever felt or imagined.

A few minutes after he had put his hooves to the ground – all four of them – Randall heard a loud bell clanging outside. It was so loud he fell on his stomach. When he got up again – on twos this time – he stepped outside out of curiosity. He half-imagined Quasimodo in the giant cottage, ringing a giant bell on Santa's command.

'Come!' Samantha appeared again, and though she wasn't flying, it looked like she was, as she was running so fast. She snatched him away and took him to an area Randall hadn't seen, one without snow. Sure, it was framed by snow-covered fir trees, but there was a race track, in a circle, where grass could be seen. Randall looked around and saw other spots, rather large ones, with grass instead of snow. Instead of snowmen and pine trees, they had bright yellow flowers.

Standing in front of the racing circle was a rather large elf. Not the one Randall almost had a laugh at, but one more lanky and thin – a dead ringer for a teenager Randall once saw working for a Santa's grotto when he was six. 'Okay,' said the elf, 'It's time for our exercises. Hey, look, it's the new guy…what's your name again?'

'Randall.'

'OK, Randall, we do this to make sure the reindeer are active. Just run about and I'll time you how long it takes for you to do three laps.' Despite the fact that Randall was never a good runner, he felt he had no choice, so he stretched and prepared himself for…

The bell.

The same bell that clanged through the village to wake everyone up. It wasn't as loud as before, but Randall still shook from the sound it caused. When the ringing in his ears finally ceased, he shook his head, took to all fours and began to dart around the racetrack, reminded of the many sports days he had in secondary school. At the end of his first lap, however, he tripped and fell to his face. He looked up, and all the response he got from that was blank stares. They looked like his mum when she was watching the soaps.

He took that as a hint, so up he went and ran again. First lap done. Now for the second, eyes on the ball. Now that that little mishap was in the past and he was actually running, he felt a strange release. As if all doubts and worries about this place, and the very fact that he was dead, instantly evaporated. His legs moved so fluidly, so naturally, Randall imagined himself as one of those cartoon characters whose legs turned into circles.

'Congratulations,' cried the elf, 'You did wonderfully.' And just like that, from nowhere the elf pulled out a little trophy.

'Um, okay,' said Randall, feeling that trying to argue with the elf would ruin the rush he just felt. He took the trophy and let the next reindeer run. The next was slow, meandering around the race track while spastically moving his legs in order to impersonate someone running. Nonetheless, he got a little trophy too.

And so did the next reindeer. And the next one. And the next one. And Samantha.

'What are you looking so grumpy for?' Samantha asked, 'You

had fun, didn't you?'

'Yeah!' replied Randall, attempting to emulate Samantha's beam. 'Had a blast!'

'Okay,' said Samantha, 'Now we're all gonna go together!'

The racetrack was big enough that all reindeer could run at the same time; so they were going to have a race. With another clang of the bell with its omnipresent ring, the reindeer were off, and though Randall felt that freedom again as he figuratively soared, Samantha was the first to finish, punctuating her victory with a 'Yay!'

They all received trophies, nonetheless.

The whole day was more or less taken up by training. Pulling a fake sleigh, using a multi-coloured treadmill, even lifting weights. Having triumphant music playing in his head did little to motivate Randall, as the smiles he was seeing had begun to increase. It was like he wasn't staring at reindeer and elves, but rather an army of robots straight out of an episode of *Doctor Who*. They distracted him, and thus he took his time in lifting the weights, but still he heard the same phrase repeating itself.

'You can do it. Come on!'

It sounded vaguely encouraging at first, but the more Randall heard it, the more it sounded like a chant used by a sinister cult. It made Randall feel like he was alive again, in that it made him want to die.

He was glad when training was over and he could go back to his nice little cottage and catch up on some reading. He took the book of fairy tales out and took a look through them. Ah, of course, it was all "happily ever after" versions. Even Randall knew the old fairy tales had been sanitised…but here he was in a fairy tale world right now.

Would he have a happy ending?

Alice remembered coming to this place. When she and Randall were dating, he couldn't wait to introduce her to his mum, Victoria. It was when he was coming over for Christmas that he invited Alice to come around for dinner, and it didn't take long for Victoria to take a liking towards Alice. When Alice mentioned that she studied history, Victoria eagerly listened as Alice discussed the life of Henry VIII and the essay she wrote on him, and Randall even proposed a toast to her and Victoria's new friendship. Then Alice and Randall watched a nice fluffy movie together, just the two of them, before they both retired for the night.

It was probably the best night they ever had as a couple.

After Randall's death, she had to come back here, if only just to say 'Hello', and to relive the memories she and Randall had shared. While she had broken up with him, and he had been a bit of a ditz, they had shared some good times together, and she simply couldn't forget him.

She rang the doorbell. She stood. The door opened.

There stood Victoria, slightly hunched over, her eyes red. 'Oh,' she said, 'Hello, Alice. I haven't seen you in a while.'

'Hello, Mrs. Smithson.'

'You're...'

'I was there when it happened,' replied Alice, wringing her hands, 'I'm sorry.'

'It's not your fault,' sighed Victoria. 'Come in.' Alice did as she was told, and as soon as she entered, Victoria collapsed onto the nearby sofa, burying her face in her hand.

'Are you okay?' asked Alice, but had no response. 'Would you like me to get you something? Would you like a cup of coffee?'

'Okay.' Alice hadn't been here for a while, and yet she still remembered where the kitchen was. The first time she came here, she baked a cake for pudding. Her favourite pudding in fact; chocolate gateau. Randall recommended it himself.

There was a Christmas garland atop the top cupboards. A little Christmas tree on one tabletop, a little snowman on another. Seeing them, Alice almost wanted to throw them in the bin; they seemed to emphasise the situation. But no, this house deserved a little touch of joy. She started making the coffee.

Two cups, a little bowl of sugar cubes. She entered the main room, seeing Victoria still sitting sadly in silence. Alice placed the tray on the coffee table and sat beside Victoria.

'Do you want to watch TV?'

'No,' said Victoria. 'I just checked. There's nothing on.' She looked away and stared at nothing, right before turning back to Alice. 'Have you been doing much recently?'

'No,' said Alice, wringing her hands. 'Just been doing my job. I...do you remember I used to do theatre? I was thinking of doing that again....or...' Alice held her stomach, feeling a pang of guilt.

'OK.' Victoria raised her head. 'Do you like acting?'

'Yeah,' said Alice, 'I...really liked the Shakespeare ones. Did you know I once played Viola in *Twelfth Night*? She's...the woman who dresses up like a man? I always thought that was one of my funniest roles.' She giggled slightly, but stopped almost instantly. Victoria chuckled a little after that. 'You know,' said Alice, 'Randall was phenomenal in that festival. He was pretty funny in his other roles too. He wanted to play Macbeth...' She stopped herself. Macbeth was a play about death, and she couldn't remind Victoria of that. The Ghost of Christmas Yet to Come represented death, and she didn't want to remind herself of that. She wanted to talk about Lenny, but she wasn't sure Victoria would want to hear it.

'Are you okay?' asked Victoria, reminding Alice of her grandma. 'You don't have to be nervous. I'm glad you came.' She looked at the floor. 'You know, Randall was utterly devastated when his father died. It was when he was about ten. He would rarely come out of his room, he would stop talking to his friends, he even got into a fight.' She looked to the Christmas tree in the corner of the room. 'It was only until about November he started acting like his old self again. He was happy at Christmas, that's what his father would have wanted.'

Hearing that made Alice feel slightly easier, and yet at the same time, made her stomach sink. 'Excuse me,' Alice said, 'I need some fresh air.'

She stepped outside and took in the icy air, which did little to soothe her, though it did remind her of Christmas, and that was something. She would go to his funeral, she would stay for a little longer to comfort his mother, it was the least she could do.

Just then, she was reminded of something else. When she was young and was alone in her dark bedroom, she would often see crawling things and monstrous figures out of the corner of her eye. She was seeing one right now; it resembled a snake with arms and legs. She turned around, and there was a man as thin and crooked as a wintry tree, decked in a porkpie hat and tweed jacket.

He turned towards her. He lifted his hat.

Randall remembered being six and excited that Santa – i.e. Mr. Doddford the headmaster – was coming to his Primary School Christmas party. Now Santa – the genuine article – was coming to his funeral. What an honour.

Randall, Samantha, the other eight reindeer and Santa were all to take a little journey to Earth to attend Randall's funeral. When Randall asked if anyone would find it weird that a group of talking deer would be in a church, Santa said that the humans would not be able to see or hear them.

Geez, what does that remind me of?

Santa forewent his Christmas sweaters and orthodox hat in favour of a black suit, and the reindeer wore black bands around their arms as well. It took a click of Santa's fingers and a little running from the reindeer and suddenly they appeared in the church Randall remembered attending.

They entered, and Randall looked about the church – and after seeing so much bright colours in Santa's land, the more placid colours of the church's walls were refreshing to his eyes. He saw Alice, he saw Lenny and saw his mother. The priest came to the podium and welcomed everyone who attended.

There was a skeleton in the audience.

Standing in the back was a living skeleton, with yellow eyeballs poking out of its skull. Was that Death? A little late wasn't...she? Yes, a she, for she was wearing a black dress and had thin cartoon eyelashes poking from its eyeballs.

'You okay?' whispered Samantha, as she turned around to see what Randall had seen. 'Oh no. What's *she* doing here?'

'Who?'

'Never mind,' she replied. 'You should be listening. This is your funeral.'

'And now,' said the priest, 'I believe Victoria, Randall's mother, would like to say a few words about her son.'

Despite the fact he had met Santa and had been bombarded with happiness and smiles, this was the first moment since his death that Randall truly felt like a child. His mum looked and sounded exactly the same as she did at his father's funeral, when Randall could hardly control himself. He sobbed right there in the church, even if it was a quieter sob than usual for him.

At his father's funeral, Mum always talked about how close Randall was to his father, and she was talking about that now. And about what high spirits Randall had, how he always found the joy in life. Randall hung his head, feeling an odd mix of honour and guilt, and then felt a hand on his shoulder. Santa's.

'I know you see the joy in life, Randall,' said Santa, 'and I know that you are willing to help me share it with everyone. Your mother is very proud of you, and I know I will be too.'

The humans cleared, and all that was left in the church were the reindeer and Santa and the skeleton. The skeleton, clasping her fleshless fingers, approached, and Randall, for whom the surprise of the skeleton had worn off, let her. That didn't stop Santa and the other reindeer from glaring at her, though.

The skeleton spoke, and her mouth moved as if she had lips. 'Santa.'

Santa still sneered. 'Diane.'

'What are you doing here?' Samantha asked.

'Well,' said Diane, her eyes narrowing for she seemed to have eyelids, 'It's just I feel a bit responsible for this man's death.' She pointed at Randall, which didn't scare Randall as much as he expected it to.

'Of course you do,' snorted Santa, the cold voice sounding strange coming out of him. 'You always see the negative side of things.'

'No,' said Diane, rubbing her temples in frustration before turning to Randall. 'I was there at the festival. You couldn't see me, but I was there. I came to see you play me.'

'So you're…'

Diane nodded, smiling a bit. 'Yes. Aren't I one of your favourite literary heroines?' Randall didn't respond. 'I saw you go out into traffic too late. I tried to save you, I ran to grab you, but…I'm sorry.'

'Leave him alone,' spat Samantha, shoving Randall away from Diane. 'Randall's still sad about his death, and the last thing he needs is you making it worse.'

'Okay, okay,' said Diane, rolling her eyes. 'I just felt…'

'What's done is done,' said Santa. 'He's with us now.'

'Yes,' added Samantha, 'In fact we'd rather have him with us, than on Earth playing you.'

Randall squirmed.

All he could do before being teleported back to the North Pole was turn to Diane and say, 'I forgive you.'

Chapter 5

'It wasn't her fault I died!' cried Randall, 'Didn't you see the video? It was my own damn fault!'

'Don't use language like that here!' said Samantha, giving Randall a little pinch. In a second, though, she calmed down and smiled. 'It's not that. No-one blames anyone for your death, Randall, but we don't want you anywhere near Diane. We worry that she may be a bad influence. After all, she's been in Purgatory for well over a century. It usually takes the souls of Purgatory less than a decade to ascend or descend.'

'How long have you been here?'

'This is my third year,' said Samantha, giggling, 'Lucky number three, Santa told me. I'm sure your day of ascension will come too, as long as Diane stays away from you and you stay away from her.'

'Well, it's just, she is supposed to be the Ghost of *Christmas* Yet to Come…'

'Exactly,' said Samantha, 'What kind of sick person would take such a joyful holiday and associate skeletons with it?'

Randall wanted to reply with, 'You know our bodies are rotting in the ground right now?' but decided against it. Santa seemed to think Samantha his favourite reindeer, so making fun of her shouldn't be done if he wanted to get into Santa's good books.

Samantha and Randall then went back into Randall's little cottage. 'I remember seeing my own funeral,' said Samantha, 'With my mum and my two little brothers. Poor Gary, poor Douglas. They ran to my coffin and were sobbing their little heads off. They were too young to really comprehend it.'

Once again, Randall found himself silent. He wanted to ask how Samantha died, but knew that wouldn't be polite here. Besides, hearing about her funeral reminded him of his own, and the tears his mother and Alice shed.

'Are you okay?'

'No, I'm fine,' said Randall as he lay on his bed. He looked at the kitchen. 'Are you staying?'

'No,' said Samantha, 'I have work to do. You should relax though, just take it easy.' She put a hand on Randall's shoulder. 'I know that seeing your funeral must be hard on you, just relax. You can even go watch a movie or even go to Toyland if you want. I can take you.'

'I'd rather stay here,' said Randall, 'Maybe catch up on some reading.' He grabbed the fairy tale book from the bookshelf, and then the *Dumbo* one. He vaguely remembered enjoying that movie.

'Okey dokey then,' said Samantha, walking away. She turned to Randall, 'Also, Santa doesn't like his helpers having sex before marriage, if you're thinking that.'

'I'm not.' Randall turned over so Samantha didn't see him flinch.

'It's just a lot of new recruits usually do,' replied Samantha. 'Have a nice day!'

She left, leaving Randall to reread the fairy tales and the Disney movie adaptation. After flicking through those, he went to the kitchen to cook himself something to eat. Not a big dinner, just little finger foods, like those his family and friends had after his funeral. His little home was bigger on the inside after all and despite the fact there seemed to be no electricity, there was even a working refrigerator. He could make himself little sandwiches, so he did, and he ate them.

But wasn't he dead, though? He once saw a ghost on TV who lamented not being able to eat. Maybe it was ghost food then? When a pig dies, does it remains ham? Even if that wasn't the case though, there was something off about the ham. Like it wasn't completely off, just a little off, or like it had been given some strange flavouring.

It was made by the hands of Santa, and he seemed to be going off or had some strange flavouring, too. Randall knew what the word "Santa" was an anagram of, and the more he pondered it, the more fitting it seemed. There was no fire and brimstone here, but the constant smiling was just as chilling.

He scratched his head, wondering if he really wanted to get away from a figure of his childhood dreams, and towards a figure of his childhood nightmares? Despite what Samantha said, he needed to see Diane again. She was the Ghost of Christmas Yet to Come, and she was real, so that must mean the other two ghosts were real as well. So were Jacob Marley and Ebenezer Scrooge, perhaps. If Toyland exists, so must Mary Quite Contrary and crooked villain Barnaby and maybe even the characters Laurel and Hardy played.

So where was Toyland? If it was close to this place, certainly Randall should have seen a giant gate or something like that. If Santa liked that land, they'd probably be forced to be happy, too. Humpty Dumpty and Little Boy Blue were tied up *Clockwork Orange*-style to watch Christmas specials.

He imagined breaking into Santa's office, beating him up and rescuing his fellow reindeer…and then descending. He wanted to ascend, so he had to do what Santa said, but he still worried that Santa might live up to his anagram. He made kids greedy, but he didn't like swearing and Randall was sure the Bible said not to swear.

He didn't know if it was the weird-tasting ham or the fact that he attended his own funeral, but Randall began to get very dizzy, and dropped off to sleep in the bed with the antler-accommodating pillows.

He awoke a few hours later – by himself, not because of a loud bell – and felt groggy as he arose. So he knew for sure that all this wasn't a dream; this was a feeling he only got when he was awake. When he woke up at about 3am due to having to piss or just because he disrupted his internal clock somehow.

What time was it now? He had no clock, and it always seemed to be night out anyway. There was always a purple sky and a full moon, but no sun, no rain, no actual blue in the sky. Still he looked outside, where he saw a shadow lurking about in the snow.

It was Diane. She was wearing a different outfit – a short grey dress with a cardigan – but despite having only met her in person for a couple of minutes, Randall could easily recognise the skull with the eyeballs and eyelashes. Seeing her made Randall burst outside and cry, 'Hey!'

Diane turned to Randall, putting a finger over her mouth. 'Sorry,' Randall whispered as Diane approached him.

'If anyone asks,' Diane whispered, 'I was never here.' She seemed to shiver.

'Look,' replied Randall as he took Diane to his cottage. 'I don't blame you for my death. Is that why you're shuddering?'

'Thank you for forgiving me,' said Diane, 'but I actually just need a fag. I can't smoke one here; Santa can sense nicotine from a hundred miles away.'

'Stone me,' said Randall, a little louder now that he was in his hovel. 'I couldn't half use a beer myself. They've got nothing to drink here except water and eggnog. I don't even know what eggnog really *is*.'

'I'd have brought you one,' said Diane, 'but Santa can sense alcohol too. He can sense anything that taints his squeaky-clean image.'

'What the he…heck? My mum always left him out a glass of sherry on Christmas Eve!'

'Well, did your mum like sherry?' laughed Diane. 'Seriously, I've been pretty worried about him.'

'Pretty?'

Diane collapsed onto Randall's bed. 'We pretty much have the same problem. No-one believes in us. People are far too cynical.'

'I've felt the same way.'

'You see, Santa has always operated in Purgatory, trying to bring joy, but I've worked on Earth on the one day of the year humans can see me.' She sighed. 'You've seen all those *Christmas Carol* movies, haven't you?'

'Yeah,' said Randall, 'Are you mad you aren't getting royalties?'

Diane actually laughed, giving Randall a little bit of pride, but then she continued, 'We've been operating long before Dickens wrote that book. A Ghost of Christmas Present is born every Christmas Eve and dies on the same night. It was originally just him that haunted those that needed to be redeemed, but they – you've heard of them, haven't you?'

'Yes.'

'They decided that adding a past and a future would be more effective. I had died about the time that decision came, so I volunteered. It was the least I could do. I even came up with the idea for my look.' She then stood up and took the duvet cover off of the bed, wrapping it around herself to create her more orthodox look. 'What I said was that since the future was unknown I should make myself unknown, hiding my face and never talking. I should also make myself look like the Grim Reaper because most of the undesirable futures involve death, I said. Really, I just hid myself because the person I first haunted wouldn't listen to a woman. It was a success, I got him to change, and I've been doing this gig ever since.'

'Has Past too?'

'No, the first Ghost of Christmas Past ascended shortly after that haunting. We're on our sixtieth. Been interesting how half of them have been men and half of them have been women, though for Charlotte and George you could hardly tell their genders.'

'So, what about Dickens…'

'It was Past No.2's idea. We have an author write a novel about us so people would be more aware of us. Our message could spread wider. Dickens seemed our best choice at the time; he needed the money, after all. He couldn't fully see or hear us but we could give him little messages in his dreams. He wrote about us, but the other characters – Scrooge and Marley and all –were his inventions. He did the book in six weeks too, that's how much we inspired him.' Dropping the duvet, Diane looked proud before sighing.

'We didn't anticipate the oversaturation. We didn't anticipate the multitude of movies, the parodies, the sitcoms and the cartoons that made us into jokes. We didn't anticipate their becoming desensitized to us. We had people dismiss us as dreams, we had people ignore us…' She stared down at the floor.

'I'm really sorry.'

'Don't be, it's not your fault. In recent years, I've had to rely on bigger things to get people's attention. I know this guy named Paul. He specialises in a lot of spectral special effects. Grabbing claws, phantom fangs, that sort of stuff. I'd show you one, but I don't want to make too much noise. I at least try to up my game, which is more than can be said for Santa.

'His goal was to lift the spirits of those of Purgatory, but most of them are too frustrated to care for his toys. He's become obsessed with reliving the past, when people believed in him enough that he could actually give presents to people on Earth. He knows there is too much cynicism and all this is his way of trying to rectify that.'

Diane shook her head. 'He's like us, you know. He's not one of them. He's a dead soul like you and me. I…I…' She collapsed again.

'What's wrong?' Randall asked, running to her.

'I was offered ascension,' she said. 'But I couldn't leave. I still had work to do. So did…Santa told me he refused ascension too.' She rose. 'Santa refused ascension,' Diane repeated, 'and I know he's beginning to regret it.' Then she laughed a bit. 'Santa and his toys. It's like Walter and his meth.'

'Wait,' said Randall, arching an eyebrow, 'you watch *Breaking Bad*, then?'

'You think I wouldn't? That show's not banned where I live. Besides, it reminds me of the type of people I have to haunt.'

'That's true,' said Randall with a small laugh.

'It's odd really,' said Diane. 'Santa talks so much about how fear has no place in Christmas, and yet we've heard of him threatening not to bring presents to naughty children. And most of the reindeer are only following orders out of fear of Hell.' Randall felt a little pang, wondering if this was the only reason he hadn't talked to Santa. 'It's a shame I can't stay,' said Diane, 'I really want to help you and the other reindeer ascend.'

'You could…' Randall racked his brains for the right words. 'Show me my future.'

'I can't,' said Diane. 'It's not Christmas Eve yet, so whatever powers I have are at their lowest. Anyway, you take care. I'll try to talk to you again if I can.' Diane let herself out, sneaking all the way. No, not sneaking, gliding.

She *was* the Ghost of Christmas Yet to Come after all. She had to be.

'Hey,' said Alice to Lenny, drumming her fingers on her Carling. 'Thanks for coming with me to the funeral.'

'It was no problem,' said Lenny as he was handed his drink. He leaned back, looking up at the ceiling. 'You know, I really wish we could have talked more. I mean, we worked at the same place, but he kept acting like I didn't exist. It was only around this time of year that he actually talked to me.'

'I think you were really the only friend he had at that place,' said Alice, staring into her drink. 'From what I heard, he was never very sociable. Oh…but he was very talkative when we were going out. He did always have some interesting things to talk about.'

'Still,' said Lenny, taking a sip of his beer. 'We should still try and have a Merry Christmas. I mean, that's what Randall would have wanted. He loved the time.'

'Yeah.' Alice stared at nothing. 'That's what his mum told me. She's a nice lady; I think I should visit her more often.'

'Yeah,' was all Lenny could say in response.

Oh god. Alice froze. There was the man again. The warped, snake-like man coming into the pub. He seemed a little less bent than

Alice remembered, but he was still wearing that jacket and hat. His frazzled hair and coke-bottle glasses reminded Alice of a cartoon mad scientist.

Though she knew better, Alice continued to stare at the bent man as he went up to the counter, standing right next to her, and ordered a drink. His voice was more or less how Alice thought it would sound; scratchy, reminding her of the sound of rats scurrying.

'Alice?' asked Lenny, 'You okay?'

Shaking her head just to wake her up, Alice turned back to Lenny. 'It's nothing. It's nothing. Sorry about that.'

The old man turned to her.

'Hello,' he said, 'Are you youngsters enjoying yourselves?'

Neither Lenny or Alice answered.

'I said, are you youngsters enjoying yourselves?' repeated the man, his voice a little lower.

'I guess,' replied Alice.

'Oh,' said the man. 'I think I saw you at the Christmas festival.' Both Alice and Lenny cringed, but they tried not to show it. 'Ah yes, I think you played Santa Claus in an adaptation of my favourite poem. You were very good, too.' He paused. 'It's a shame what happened to that young man.'

'Randall? He was a friend of ours,' Alice asked. 'So, do you live around here?'

'I just moved,' replied the old man. 'Oh, he was your friend, was he? That must have been hard on you. What would you say if he could be brought back to life?'

'What are you talking about?'

'I just know someone who's been dabbling in that sort of thing. It sounds very interesting. I'm sure you'd like it if your friend was resurrected, and I'm certain he'd like it too.'

With a small shudder, Lenny took Alice by the hand and moved her to another table. The old man stayed where he was, but managed to flick a little card in their direction, which strangely fluttered right onto the table they had sat at.

'Would you believe that guy?' said Lenny, with a slight whisper. 'He was like a *Scooby Doo* villain, he was.'

Alice said nothing. She picked up the card.

Barnaby, it said.

Chapter 6

When Randall was called to collect from Toyland, the first thing he asked was what differentiated Toyland from Santa's home. He was told that only people who die at Christmas and who had a special affection for Christmas were given duties at Santa's workshop, while Toyland was open to the souls of the dead all year round. The souls that went to Toyland were those of children – even they had to prove they were worthy of Heaven – and those who entertained children. Authors of children's books, creators of children's cartoons, hosts of children's TV. Elves made toys, yes, but the denizens of Toyland not only made toys, they wrote new books, performed new music and recorded new video. *Ollie's Funhouse* may have been cancelled on Earth, but new episodes had been made for the kids – and the baby boomers – of Purgatory. Only now Ollie was a giant talking cat, which many viewers said was an improvement.

Like Randall had been turned into a reindeer, many of the residents of Toyland had taken on the forms of nursery rhyme and fairy tale characters. So Mary Quite Contrary didn't originally go by that names, but had adopted it when she arrived at Toyland; Randall didn't ask, but he assumed Barnaby had that name when he was alive. The story of the opera happened, and it seemed Santa inspired Victor Herbert to tell the tale.

Randall expected Samantha to be accompanying him, but she thought it was time he did something on his own. He couldn't ascend unless he knew how to be independent, she said, but she helped a little by telling him where Toyland could be found. It was beyond the great pine tree forest; all he had to do was walk until there was no more snow – hearing this reminded Randall of how much he had begun to enjoy the taste of grass.

So off Randall went by himself into the pine tree forest, and when he did, the combination of the wind and the rows and rows of snow-covered trees made him feel a tinge – just a tiny tinge – of the Christmas magic this place should have had.

The more Randall walked, the more the snow began to fade, and white made way for green. The blue sparkles were soon replaced by pink flowers, and of course, little teddy bears and dolls. Before long, he saw a giant purple gate, framed by two toy soldiers. Suddenly, the thought that someone died and got made into a toy soldier hit Randall, but then he remembered the play and the Laurel and Hardy movie – *March of the Wooden Soldiers* – and thus came to the conclusion that these guards must have been built. They weren't dead because they were never alive to begin with; when he thought about it, Randall didn't know which option was the most disturbing.

The toy soldiers, with a creak, looked downwards and observed Randall. Randall almost expected them to shoot a red beam to scan him, but instead, the soldiers merely saluted and said 'Servant of Santa, you are welcome here.'

The gates creaked open and Randall steeled himself to look upon something wondrous. He closed his eyes while entering, and opened them to behold what looked no different from the many kiddie theme parks he had seen in his life. The houses were all built in a medieval peasant style, and were made out of plastic, some of them having the paint chipping away. The trees weren't real, they were enlarged Lego pieces – *well, a dead person wouldn't need oxygen, but still.*

There was life to be found in the plaza; two Humpty Dumpties. Two of them, both dressed in clothes that looked more like wrapping paper. They looked like eggs…somewhat. They had no shell, rather they had flesh. Two giant bald heads with tiny eyes and a big mouth, attached to little arms and little legs. They reminded Randall of how Humpty Dumpty looked in *Through the Looking Glass*, with all those wrinkles and things that made him look real and unreal. They were political caricatures given flesh. There was a skull under there. There was a brain. No yolk, no chicken.

One of them approached Randall.

'Hi!' the egg said, holding out his hand, which looked like that of a baby. Randall shook it, but it felt like it wasn't done out of choice.

'Hello,' said Randall, scratching the back of his neck, 'My name's Randall. I'm here for the goodies for Santa.'

'I know you are,' said the Humpty. 'Pleased to meet you. My name is Lawrence Hudson. You may have heard of my work.'

'Oh yes,' replied Randall, 'I read...' He was about to say 'I read your books when I was a kid', for he had the entire collection of *Ernie Erstweiler* books about the young detective, with Hudson's photo on the back of every one of them. This person, this Humpty, looked almost exactly like that photo, only squashed and stretched and moving. When his face moved, it reminded Randall of those morphing programs he used to goof around with.

'You must be new,' said Hudson, laughing a bit. 'You're scared of how I look. Don't be. I mean, I'm nothing compared to descending.'

Randall gulped, his possible fate springing into his brain.

'Anyway, my latest book is complete. Let me tell you, writing it was the easy part, but editing was a nightmare. Nonetheless *Ernie Erstweiler and the Werewolf's Waistcoat* is ready to distribute come Christmas Eve.'

Hudson beckoned Randall to come into his plastic pseudo-Medieval house, where boxes and boxes of Ernie's latest escape were waiting to be delivered.

'OK,' said Randall, growing slightly more used to whatever the Humpty was. The flesh egg. It was quite amusing actually.

'Great,' said Hudson, and he handed Randall a pile of boxes, which Randall held in his hoof-hands. The boxes reached up to his antlers, and he kept them still by holding them up to one of the little prongs. Unfortunately, this now meant the boxes were blocking his vision, and thus he spent some time stumbling about Toyland before crashing into a plastic wall. Hudson laughed. 'On second thought, try two piles at a time.'

Randall felt like hitting himself on the head for not thinking of that, but went along with it anyway. One little pile that rested under his chin, one that he could take back to Santa while keeping his vision, and more importantly, one he could run with. He darted through the wintry forest, dropped them off at the workshop, rinse and repeat.

'Nice work, Randall,' said Santa, picking up the books. 'The kids will love these...hmmm. Werewolf?'

'I had a quick flick through it,' said Randall, 'The werewolf is just misunderstood. He just wants to make friends. It's really touching.'

'Oh ho,' said Santa, 'Okay. I've just been a little concerned about some of the product that's come out of there. Ollie did sneak in something I wasn't sure of in one of his DVDs.'

'Well, didn't you say we were distributing these to adults as well?'

'Yes, but the last thing these poor souls need is to be reminded of the misery that exists in both life and the afterlife. What they need is to be reminded of the joy only childhood can bring. I mean, is that not the reason you enjoy our Christmas specials?'

'Yeah,' replied Randall. 'I guess that is the reason. I'm just a big kid. You know…I was in the entertainment centre recently and saw a film called *The Lonely Yeti.*'

'Oh, that's a good movie.'

'It has a yeti who everyone is afraid of because he looks scary, and you help him make friends and I just thought…' That twinkle in Santa's eye seemed to fade. 'Never mind. There's nothing else you want me to fetch from Toyland?'

Duppyville looked just like any town would. In fact, it was just a normal town, just with ghosts and ghouls. The souls whose duties were the ones they did in life; postmen who died worked as postmen here, janitors who died worked as janitors here.

And in a bungalow, behind a garden filled with a variety of flowers and one or two gnomes, there lived the Ghost of Christmas Yet to Come.

People – or Purgatory's equivalent of people - had asked her why she didn't live in a fancy house due to her celebrity status. They did have money after all. Nonetheless, she was never one to ask for much, and as she liked to remind people, this was Purgatory, not Heaven.

If this wasn't Purgatory, she wouldn't have to do her duty.

She put on her most famous outfit – the dark black robe that hid her face, leaving only her skeletal hands exposed. Closing her eyes, she imagined herself away from her bright home and near the unmourned grave of one of her clients. It's not just pointing at things, she reminded herself, there's an art to body language.

But that was what people were expecting, wasn't it? Her clients had all heard the story before, they knew what to expect. Last year, Paul had given her a device that made her look like the Devil; people still feared the Devil, didn't they? Turns out that made her client less likely to listen to her.

Still, she had to drive herself into people's minds, make sure they always remembered her. That used to be so easy, but then again, Diane felt she should have a challenge to keep herself alert. She was the ghost of the future, after all, and she knew the world was always changing. How long had she been doing this, two centuries? Three? There had been so many changes – new technology, new attitudes, new Ghosts of Christmas Past and Present – and she had made sure that she fully understood every one of them.

Yes, she had been doing this for centuries, and she'd do it for centuries more. A woman's work is never done went the old saying, and there were always people Diane wanted to help. Every person she was told to help, she wanted to help. All this spectacle, all this horror, it was for their own good. Candy canes and fluffiness were nothing without fear of punishment, without fear of dying alone.

Diane pulled down her hood, collapsed onto her bed and pulled out a cigarette. She had never smoked when she was alive, only having discovered the wonders of nicotine after death when its effects didn't matter. That was the thing about the afterlife: you got more chances to do the things you've always wanted to.

That is, unless you've ended up at Santa's.

She had just been there, to talk to that reindeer who dressed up as her before his death, so what was stopping her from just going up to Santa and talking to him? Well, there was the fact he shared a flaw with many of her clients; he didn't listen. He didn't want to change. He was happy trying to force happiness.

But she would talk to him. She would talk to him again. But not today. She had to practice today. Then she had to meet with Paul about what to use for the big night. Then go to the pub to talk with Marcus Forshaw, the newest Ghost of Christmas Past. Why didn't Santa's land have any pubs? Maybe the reindeer and elves would be less stressed come December 24th.

Diane put the hood back on. No, she couldn't jettison the hood and robe. She did have some successes while wearing those things, didn't she? She taught that one man not to spoil his daughter, didn't she? Besides, she was far too attached to these clothes. Though she resembled Death, wearing this garb made her feel truly alive. Putting it on rendered her silent, yet she felt she could drive a message better than before.

Another practice session. More pretending that the big night had come and she was not in her humble bungalow, but rather on Earth, in a future that may be. She was the embodiment of terror, the dark shadow that lurked in the corners. And she had some new tricks up her sleeve; she stretched her fingers and made her form skinnier with the small amount of power she had in December. She recalled all the horror movies and PSAs she had watched for research, and had tried to emulate them. With Paul's help, of course.

What a coincidence. Just when she was thinking of Paul, her mobile phone's alarm started to beep, reminding her of the meeting she was supposed to have with Paul. Thus she threw off her robe – before putting it on a hanger, of course – and put on a dress with a belt, as well as tights and furry boots. Humans, always thinking of nice-looking outfits.

With her wardrobe sorted, Diane walked off towards Paul's shop, which of course he called 'The Little Shop of Horrors'. He should have been glad copyright laws were more lax in Purgatory. Paul had been a special effects guru in life, and often fancied himself visiting the worlds he created. When he died, he went to Purgatory, which gave him more toys to play with, more worlds to create. He sold his wares to those who needed a wake-up call, those who wanted to shoot a movie or put on a play or just those who were looking for a practical joke to play. He had been active fairly recently, but long enough to make Diane wonder why he had neither ascended nor descended by now.

His shop was probably the one thing in Duppyville that, if you forgot what Purgatory was really like, really did look like it came from the afterlife. A giant skull head with bat wings, silently roaring at Diane as she entered. Paul was even the orthodox bedsheet ghost so often seen in popular culture. Those were rarer around here than both Paul and Diane would have liked.

He sat behind a counter, in front of a variety of zombie limbs and skulls, drumming his fingers until Diane came in. At that, he sprung to life, clasping his hands together. 'Ah, Diane. Good to see you.'

'Okay,' said Diane, folding her arms. 'What have you got for me?'

'I'm glad you asked,' said Paul, pulling out a box. 'You told me that one of the clients you have booked is the miserly CEO of a shoe company, so why not try this out for size?' He opened the box and out popped a mass of floating shoes, with snakes instead of laces, little spider legs on their soles, and faces like that of Munich's *Scream*. 'You have disgraced us,' moaned the shoes, 'Now you must pay the price.'

'Hmm. I dunno.'

'Or,' said Paul, 'How about the Barefoot Banshee?' He pulled out another box, and out popped a fake ghost in a tattered white robe, showing off its naked feet. 'Your wares are useless in Hell,' it shrieked.

'Well, we don't want him to stop selling shoes.'

'Ah,' said Paul, 'but we do want him to see that there's more to life than shoes!'

'Yes, but that banshee thing seems more like it was meant for some fetish rather than to teach someone a lesson.'

Paul giggled nervously.

'Oh, don't get all worked up,' moaned Diane, rubbing her head. 'I'll take the evil shoes.'

'Okay,' said Paul. 'Now, you say you've also got a sex maniac who needs to be taught women aren't objects? Well, have I got...'

Just then, another customer came in. It – for Diane and Paul couldn't tell which gender it was – reminded Diane of the fictional Scrooge, with its gigantic top hat and coat, both of which hid its face somewhat. It seemed to be something like what Paul was, as Diane could see a bit of white under its hat.

'Boo!' it said. 'I want to build a haunted attraction, and I want to know what you've got.'

'Um,' said Diane, 'That's a bit redundant, isn't it?'

'No, no,' said Paul, 'I still like haunted attractions even after becoming a ghost, though I must admit it's a bit out of season.'

'Oh, you can have them any time!' said the figure, raising its hands in delight. 'Besides, Christmas is a time for celebration, and I can think of no better way to celebrate then terrifying the wits out of people! Isn't that right, Diane?'

Diane raised an eyebrow, or at least did the equivalent of that gesture. 'What's that supposed to mean?'

The figure didn't reply, but rather gave Paul a wad of money, and Paul gave the figure a brief tour of some of his more popular wares. Still having her doubts, Diane sat down on a nearby chair, and had a quick look around herself. Hmm, tentacles. Never tried that before.

So that was all the books, then, thought Randall, as he retired back to his cottage. *Strange that they should come from Toyland, but then again, books can be toys, can't they, if you build a little tower with them or throw them at people? Then again, if toys got a land, then why not books? Everything should have a land, like, imagine if there was a Shoeland.*

Then Randall wondered whether or not to call the entirety of Purgatory Bookland, given that he had recently been engaged in conversation with a character from Dickens, and of course, he was an animal featured in countless storybooks. During his time in Purgatory, he heard his fellow reindeer refer to their new home as "The North Pole" but Randall didn't see that as an appropriate name. They didn't live on Earth; they didn't even deliver presents on Earth.

But they did go to Earth, Randall had heard. They had gone down to Earth on Christmas Eve when humans could see them, but had also delivered messages to humans without being seen.

Could I do that?

As soon as Randall thought of that, he planned out on his head how to do it. He had seen so many ghosts in movies and TV shows do things like that with ease. They just walked through walls, just made things float about. Randall couldn't go through the cottage walls – they were Purgatory walls and thus made from the same spooky material he was now. But if Diane and her friends could inspire Dickens and Santa inspired Herbert, Randall had a hunch he could share his story too. He could go to his Mum and Alice and even Lenny, just to let them know he was still out and about somewhere.

He would think about his flat, and then would teleport there. Then he would walk about with his arms in front and moan and rattle about chains...

Jacob Marley wore chains as punishment for his sins. He was forced to carry the weight of his long-doings for all eternity, and was reminded of all the good he could have done in life. Now that Randall knew that *A Christmas Carol* was based on actual characters, he couldn't help but imagine the same thing happening to him. He imagined the same thing happening to him just for going home. After all, Santa didn't want his reindeer going anywhere else in Purgatory, why would he want them to go to Earth for non-funeral-related reasons?

Santa had been showing up less and less; maybe Samantha would know the rules about going to Earth. She was always kissing Santa's ass, and seemed to know more than he did. After a quick sandwich – as off as it was – he would go and ask her. Maybe she'd give him some more advice on how to ascend or could talk some more about this world's origins.

He stepped outside, and he saw Samantha hobbling about the snow, carrying a sack. 'Hey!' he cried, which made Samantha drop the sack instantly.

'Oh, it's you again,' said Samantha. 'It seems we keep running into each other, doesn't it?'

'What's that?' asked Randall, pointing to the sack.

She smiled again. That wide, freaky smile that would creep out the Cheshire Cat. 'More things from Toyland!' she said, holding out another book.

'It doesn't have werewolves, does it?'

She put the book back in the sack, laughing. 'No, but it's by another Humpty.'

'Those?' said Randall, 'Do you think those are creepy?' Stupid question.

'How can you say that?' said Samantha, 'I'd have thought you'd have gotten used to being a reindeer by now. Remember, you've got to have high spirits for the big night! We're not the Ghost of Christmas Yet to Come!'

Randall forced a laugh. 'Hey,' said Randall, 'I was just wondering. When we went to the funeral, I never got a chance to really interact with Mum or Alice or my friends. Since Christmas is getting closer, I was wondering if I can go visit them.'

'They won't be able to see or hear you until Christmas Eve, you realise that.'

'Well, it's just, didn't Santa say that he inspired the play of *Babes in Toyland* through dreams or something?'

'Santa is a more powerful spirit than you. He has been here several years while you have only just got here. You may see your family and friends,' said Samantha, a small tic in her eye, 'but they may not be able to see you is all I am saying. Please do not be disappointed.'

'Okay,' said Randall. 'Seeing my mum and her not seeing me is better than not seeing her at all, and…' He chortled to himself. 'Imagine if she saw me like this anyway.' Though Randall expected Samantha to get offended at what he said, she laughed too.

'I know how you feel,' said Samantha, placing a hoof-hand on Randall's shoulder. 'I was scared and confused too, you know. When I was doing all these jobs for Santa, I couldn't help but wonder what my family would think of me now. My dad always wanted me to follow in his footsteps; I doubted he'd be thrilled to see me as a reindeer.'

'Oh, don't talk about fathers,' said Randall, rubbing his

forehead. 'Anyway, how do I go to Earth?'

'You just focus,' said Samantha, 'You just focus.'

'Thought so,' was Randall's reply. 'Hey, did you visit your family much?'

'No,' sighed Samantha, slumping. 'I just...I just didn't have the guts. But that's okay.' She stood upright and beamed again. 'This place has everything I could want! And if I ever feel sad or lonely, Santa is always willing to talk to me. Maybe you should see him m-'

'Okaythanksbye.' With that, Randall zoomed away as quick as if he were on that racetrack, back to his home. So his hunch was confirmed. He could transport himself to his mother's house or Rob's house or Alice's house. What was better, Santa was okay with that, and so was Samantha. All he had to do was focus and for a while, he'd be back at his house. Back with his mother. Just for a little while. Just long enough to say goodbye.

But he didn't.

'Well, of course I thought he was crazy at first, but then I remembered advertising. A lot of TV ads are intentionally weird so the viewers will remember the advert better and thus remember the product better. If we use surreal images, people will remember our visits better, and thus remember the message better. I mean, one thing I want people to think is, "You're so mean we went through all this trouble just to change your ways. You're getting a big spectacle because that's what you deserve."'

That's what Diane said as she sat on her bar stool, bony legs crossed, as she stared at her most recent Ghost of Christmas Past. This one was a male, a young man with a slight resemblance to Anthony Perkins, wearing a rather baggy business suit. Diane suggested he wear a suit to the haunting, just so the client knew they meant business. At least a better fitting one.

'I don't know,' said Marcus, for that was the ghost's name. 'You said one of the problems we had was that people kept thinking our visitations were dreams. Surely they'll think it's a dream if we have evil shoes.'

'Maybe,' said Diane, 'but Paul knows what he's doing. You've got to admit, he's pretty talented when it comes to this stuff.'

'Well, I would think this stuff would be easy to do here,' replied Marcus. 'Hell, you could even try making this sort of thing yourself. You are the most terrifying Christmas icon of them all, after all.'

Despite feeling slightly flattered, Diane moaned. 'I've tried, you know. It didn't come out too well. I mean, I died before we had good tools for special effects. Paul was born with that type of stuff.'

'And do you really think we need him if we're supposed to be at our most powerful on Christmas Eve?'

'Well, we may be able to show the past and future, but I don't think…' Diane noticed Marcus staring at his drink forlornly. 'Oh, come on, don't be Mr. Self-Doubt-And-Loathing. We have enough of them here.'

'Didn't you say we were having troubles converting people?'

'We've had successes recently though! Don't you know the last Ghost of Christmas Past ascended upon his first success? Just think, this year, you could ascend in just a few days!'

Marcus snorted.

'What?'

'If it's that easy, why hasn't it happened to you yet? Why are you still here?'

'I'm here because I want to be,' replied Diane. 'Because there's people that need my help.'

'Doesn't Santa hate us?' moaned Marcus, looking away. 'I liked Santa when I was a kid, I don't want him to hate me.'

'I wouldn't take him seriously,' said Diane, 'It's me he really hates. I'm sure he has nothing against you. He doesn't like me because he doesn't want Christmas associated with the Grim Reaper, but you don't dress as the Grim Reaper. He likes whimsy and the first time I met you, you had a pretty whimsical character. You were excited about this job. What happened?'

'I guess I just thought a bit more about it, really,' said Marcus. 'It's like, you know when you're a kid and you want to be like Jackie Chan, but then you find out there's a lot of work to do in karate and that stuff?'

'You know,' said Diane, 'I have wanted to try karate for a while, actually. Not sure how effective I'd be at though, since I am a skeleton.'

'Anyway,' said Marcus, his eyes narrowing. 'I remember when I was a kid I watched the Muppet version of *Christmas Carol* – *That* one again, thought Diane – 'and I wanted to give that sort of treatment to my headteacher. He was always having a go at me. I wanted to give him what for.'

'We're not doing this for revenge, you know.'

'I know, that was when I was a kid.'

'This job isn't as hard as some people think it is. I mean, really, you have the least to do. It's mostly me and this year's Present that they depend on to bring the change.'

Marcus said nothing, and finished off his Guinness.

'You know,' said Diane, 'I read somewhere that beer is supposed to help you be more creative. Two beers to help clear the mind, and two coffees to help keep you alert and awake.'

'Creative?'

'Yes, we're always requiring new techniques and new ideas. We're not like Santa, who insists on using the same old workshop and same old methods.' Diane sighed. 'You know one of his new reindeer?'

'What about him?'

'Never mind. Hey, would you like me to walk you home?' He stared. 'Not for that reason, you pervert,' Diane added half-jokingly.

'Okay,' replied Marcus, and after a couple more beers, they went outside. Before they went off, Diane had a quick fag; she asked Marcus if he wanted one and he said he didn't smoke even in death. After that, she took him home. He lived in a bungalow not too dissimilar from Diane's if not a little smaller.

'You know,' said Diane, 'I have a house like this. You ever hear the old joke?'

'The one where he runs out of bricks and says...'

'I'll bung a low roof on it,' the two ghosts said in unison. They laughed and put their arms around each other like drunken old friends. They entered, and Diane took a look around. The living room was a moderate one, not big enough for a party or anything like that, but had a TV and a sofa and some potted plants.

'You see,' said Diane, 'They wouldn't give a house like this to any ghost, now would they? Look at the accommodations Santa's helpers get. All filthy wooden houses, and they're not allowed to complain.'

'I know Santa's leery of us,' said Marcus, 'but do you have to keep talking about him? I get it; he runs his world very badly. You told me not to take him seriously, yet here you are complaining about him. What did he ever do to you?'

Diane flinched, but replied, 'Very well. Let's talk about something else.'

He had always hated children. Now that he knew magic and supernatural forces existed, he hated them even more.

When he was alive, he had authored a series of books about a duck named Edward. A duck that was basically human, one who wore a top hat, carried a cane with his wings and attended social parties. Barnaby had meant the series to be one for adults- he only used a duck because he knew a man who looked like a duck - but then he remembered that children liked cute little animals, and that children's literature was popular, and that books kept the little brats quiet.

Edward The Duck Goes To The Ball. Edward The Duck In Court. They were bestsellers and made Barnaby a good amount of money, but that sort of fame does come with a price. "The Author of Edward the Duck" was his title throughout life, with his other works, his anthologies and poetry going forgotten. He used to write about the beauty of nature and the evils of upper class, but he was solely remembered for his children's books.

It carried on even in death. He died in his sleep, and since his most well-known work was a children's book, he ended up in Toyland. He at first thought it a strange dream, but no, it was his assignment. Not only was he to write more *Edward* books, he had to do it in the guise of the Crooked Man from the famous nursery rhyme. He was even given a cat to play with and a house that reminded him of the Leaning Tower as drawn by Tim Burton.

And there were children there too. Barnaby wished he could feel sympathy for those who had left the mortal plane so young, but he couldn't leave his house without being bombarded by them. The new *Edward* books he wrote were only done so he would have a chance at ascension, and thus he didn't put as much effort into them as he did earlier works, yet the children ate up *Edward The Duck Makes A Sandwich* and squabbled at him how good it was. It was him they seemed to pick on most; even the Humpties laughed at him.

Even in death, he thought, he needed respect. Being made into the creepy Crooked Man couldn't have done him any favours; he had heard of how Santa viewed that Grim Reaper lookalike. Mary Mary Quite Contrary, as she preferred to be known, had a fair amount of popularity, and was looked upon fondly for her plays, so Barnaby thought that if he would woo her and marry her, some of that respect would rub off on him.

It was after she overlooked him for that one macho idiot that Barnaby realised how meaningless Toyland really was. Why bother to force sentiment and saccharine onto dead children? If they were dead, Barnaby told people, they should realise how harsh the world really is and those who don't are too stupid to deserve presents anyway. Also, just because people wrote for children didn't mean they deserved to be in a childish place; understanding what a child wants from his entertainment actually requires maturity. So ascension and descent be darned, he was going to destroy Toyland and everything it stood for.

Not too far from Toyland was the Dark Forest. This was supposed to be a place where people could cleanse their sins by confessing them loudly and by being punished by ghouls. Ghouls were never people. They weren't dead or alive. They were skeletal, humanoid beings with small amounts of fur covering their bodies and their only instinct was to cause harm. As soon as they saw someone, they bit and chewed and tugged and various other nasty things, thus people were told to exercise caution when using them to atone.

Well, if their purpose was to help cleanse sins, then shouldn't everyone in Purgatory have to encounter them? If they didn't have sin, Barnaby said, then they would have gone to Heaven straight away. So when Barnaby met two of his young fans, he led them to the Dark Forest, believing he was doing them all a favour. He was showing them the true purpose of Purgatory. That this place wasn't supposed to be all sugar and sunshine. Even if he did descend, he thought, he had made a point.

He had found another person who was sick of the cheeriness of the realm, and he was a Toymaker. He and Barnaby thus collaborated on creating an army of vicious toys that would go about Toyland, destroying everything in their path. This, they both reasoned, would cause people to shun childish things, as they would be so frightened of them. So out into the streets went the cackling jack-in-the-boxes and the fanged teddy bears, growling and snarling…only the citizens of Toyland immediately disposed with them. 'This isn't the first time someone has done this,' Barnaby was told by a Toyland resident.

After the evil toys were defeated and the children rescued, Barnaby…well…

Though he had prepared himself for the fire and devils, what followed for the next few years were reminders. Reminders that he had something that made children happy, but threw it all away for his own selfish reasons. Reminders that he had tried to destroy a land of innocence simply because of his own reputation. Accusations being hammered in his head. Guilt being forced into him. A trial that went on and on and on.

Not only that, but another constant reminder was that his little escapade inspired a whole play. Every performance of the play, every movie adaptation wormed its way into his brain, transforming him into a ridiculous cartoon supervillain, draining every drop of his dignity.

And of course, he had chains around him. Chains representing his lost potential, his selfish actions, his hatred of children, even. At least he could be honest here.

Most people in Hell had no concept of time, but Barnaby knew all too well when it was Christmas Eve, the day of his descent. Halloween and Christmas Eve were when souls were at their strongest, and those were the times the souls tried to escape from Hell, and when "they" were at their most vigilant. It was the whole purpose of Halloween traditions, Barnaby had heard, to keep souls in Hell. The pumpkins and the costumes were originally made to scare the souls that had escaped, but it was only Christmas when Barnaby attempted his escape. Normally they would find him and bring him back into the pits, but one year he had managed to creep past when they were busy with another escaping soul.

He had found a crack and had squeezed and scrooged – no pun intended – his way back into Purgatory. The chains he wore were not only supposed to be reminders of his misdeeds in life, but were also supposed to slow him down were he to escape and so that he could easily be spotted. How fortunate for him, then, that the first figure he met upon reaching Santa's home was a reindeer that showed him a path to Earth. He'd still be invisible to mortals, but at least he'd have more places to hide. They were powerful, but they weren't omniscient.

So he couldn't be seen. He couldn't be heard. Nonetheless, the barrage of accusations, guilt and poorly-made movies had ended, and he could finally think about other things. He could think of how to get back at them and Toyland and Santa. Though he did consider what he would do to Mary and her husband, he knew that they had both ascended shortly after their marriage and even he couldn't penetrate Heaven. Yet Santa, he who Mary was making toys for, had not ascended and seemingly never would. Neither had the Ghost of Christmas Yet to Come, who was doing the same thing to others what Hell had done to him. The voices of Hell compared him to Scrooge, so the fact that characters from that story actually existed gave him a form of post-mortem nausea.

Once again he started hearing voices in his head, but not the voices from Hell (whatever those were, he thought, they were worse than little men in red jumpsuits). No, it was his rescuer. The one who had showed him the other crack and led him to Earth, and now it was leading him to another place. A medium's, not too far from a rickety shopping district. Even after acknowledging the existence of ghosts and the afterlife, it did give Barnaby that nausea again. He only entered because it was at the behest of his saviour.

When he floated – or walked, it felt like walking – in, he saw two men sat at a table, eying a tiny pyramid. They reminded him of two people who aided him in his Toyland invasion – the fact that he never saw them again was the only positive he could find in Hell. The closer he came to the pyramid, the more he felt a new type of nausea; a rather pleasant one at that.

'We sense you,' said the shorter of the two men. 'And we sense that you have been brought here to participate in our experiment.'

Experiment? From having his brain filled up with so many cartoons in Hell, Barnaby knew the connotations of that word and would have floated off if the taller one had not spoken.

'We know what's to be found in Purgatory. Santa lives there. His elves and reindeer live there. Toyland's there and the Ghosts of Christmas are there.'

Barnaby stayed almost instinctively. The two men were brothers, and had a sort of fascination with Christmas. Or an anti-fascination, rather. They had been exposed to the fact that Santa didn't operate on Earth early at about age six, when they caught sight of their mum and dad getting the presents out of a cupboard. The shorter one, Carl, asked what they were doing and their Dad just spilled the beans right there and then, with Carl and brother Derek parroting those words all over the playground.

Later, when they were much older, they were both in a car accident on Christmas Eve and spent Christmas in a coma. Though they had little interaction with what they saw, they saw Santa's workshop and how it was run. They saw the alcohol being shunned in favour of cocoa and milk, they saw the children's cartoons playing on TVs with no news or talk shows to be found. They even caught a quick glimpse of the Ghosts of Christmas planning their haunting.

Their early revelation had meant that they had a critical eye for the commercialism and simplification of Christmas. A holiday of stress and anguish hiding under a guise of something banal and jolly. Carl and Derek had delved into the occult for many reasons – to speak with the dead, to discover secrets, to make money – but another reason was to find Santa Claus and dismantle his image. That way, the rusty cogs of the holiday would be exposed.

'Ah-ha!' cried Derek as he peered into the pyramid. 'I'm sensing…this is the crooked man Barnaby! You would make a fine ally! Come, come!'

Their experiment? It was an arcane spell they had uncovered that was said to bring the dead back to life. They had tried to use it while just thinking about a certain spirit, but it yielded no results. Then they realised they needed an actual spirit in the room with them to get any progress.

Barnaby was told to stand in the middle of the room while Carl took out the spell and read it. He felt another brand of nausea – a mixture between the "bad" one and the "good" one, as he writhed and shook.

A skeleton began to form near – on him. When the leg bones materialised, they were his leg bones. Even though the hip and the spine hadn't formed, he could still move the legs about. It didn't take long for the rest of the bones to form, and as soon as they had formed, entrails began to grow inside the bones. Long intestine, short intestine, lungs, stomach.

Then the muscles crawled all around the bones and organs, and before Barnaby could welcome his precious flesh, his vision was clouded by a bright white light.

When the light cleared, he heard a sound emanating from himself, something hoarse, something rough…he was breathing! Though he still closed his eyes – in case something had gone wrong and he had transformed into some hideous abomination- he ran his fingers over his skin. Yes, his skin was there. Still wrinkled, but it was there. And- and his favourite bedrobe too. So the spell reverted him back to the state in which he died in.

'You don't have any spells that make me younger, do you?' asked Barnaby, opening his eyes. He looked as he did the day he died, same age, same clothes, same frizzled hair. Though if he died in this state…

'Fraid not,' replied Carl. 'But hopefully the magic we used should make you a little more active then you were before you died.'

'I'm glad you were willing to co-operate, really,' said Derek, as he looked over the spell, 'This spell requires the spirit to be ready to be resurrected. If it wants to remain dead, it stays dead.'

'And who would want to remain dead?' spat Barnaby.

'You have been to Purgatory, haven't you?' said Carl, 'Some

people are determined to stay there until they ascend. I bet they think of it as some sort of video game. And then we have Santa who doesn't want to leave Purgatory ever so he can continue delivering his piss-poor presents to the masses.'

'Calm yourself, Carl,' said Derek, patting Carl on the shoulder. 'Remember, we do have something else planned for Santa.'

Carl and Derek had offered Barnaby asylum in their home, and had given him some new clothes as well so he could fit in more. Sadly, he retained some of the crookedness he had in Toyland, but very few people seemed to notice, and even if they did, they likely wouldn't think anything weird of it.

He had lasted longer than he thought he would in his new body; a whole week. When that week was over, he and Carl and Derek had gained contact with another spirit: the reindeer that had led Barnaby to the crack. Yes, she knew her way about Santa's land and had done what so few of his servants had while still keeping herself in Santa's good books.

'Samantha,' said Barnaby. 'Good to see you.'

'Ah,' said Samantha, who could be heard, but not seen. 'So he was a success, was he?'

'Yes,' said Carl, smiling. 'Are you here to have the same happen to you?'

'Not yet, not yet,' said Samantha. Though Barnaby couldn't see her, he could tell she was waving her hands about. 'I've still got to get others to agree to this. I think I've found a potential in the new reindeer, Randall, his name is. Barnaby's been to his neighbourhood and has found his friends and family still miss him.'

'Oh,' said Derek, looking over the spell. 'No can do. It worked for Barnaby because he had been dead for so long. It shouldn't work if he died just this year. How long have you been dead?'

'Hmmm,' snorted Samantha, 'I doubt it'd be long enough for it to work now. But it should work on Christmas Eve without limits, that's what matters.'

'Well, yeah, it should,' said Carl.

'Shame,' said Derek, 'I would have liked to cripple Santa sooner. His elves and reindeer are probably like five years at most. This spell needs about half a century or so.

'Christmas Eve should be more than enough time to do what we want to do,' said Samantha. 'What's more important is whether or not you've got the containment ready.'

'Yeah,' said Carl. 'I think so.'

'No,' snarled Derek, 'We still have some things to work out there.'

'Oh yeah,' replied Carl.

Barnaby sighed, rubbing his forehead. 'They're just like the help I had back in Toyland, aren't they?'

'Yes,' replied Samantha, 'Still, credit where credit is due, they are doing what they're supposed to do, and doing it quite well, too. Now if you excuse me, I'm off.'

So the pyramid stopped glowing and Derek and Carl set off to create the containments Samantha requested, with Barnaby even stepping in to help them a bit. After all the childish literature he had had to endure, reading about resurrecting the dead and arcane magic was refreshing.

Meanwhile, in a place not too far from the forest that led to Toyland but still not a place Santa wanted his elves and reindeer scarpering off to, Samantha stood, dusting off her body. She looked back at the forest, as fake to her as the Christmas theme park she attended as a kid. Though she said she believed in this world, it was now making her as nauseous as Barnaby was when he was in Hell. After staring a while at her hooves, knowing that they'd disappear soon, she darted back into the woods, unaware someone else was darting off with her.

Chapter 7

Once again Randall felt a strange urge to wake up for no real reason. He'd be slowly dragged out of a peaceful sleep back into the real world…if this place could be called the real world. Every time he woke up, he still expected to open his eyes and find himself back in his flat, alive and kicking and among normal people. No, every time he woke up, he saw his little kitchen, his bookshelf, the paintings of snowy landscapes hanging from his walls.

Also, out of his window was a certain skeleton, the eyes shifting back and forth. Her again? Actually, seeing her gave him a slight feeling of relief, given that she wasn't some constantly-smiling cute cartoon animal. He opened the door and let her in, and she stumbled in, almost looking like she would fall apart – Randall didn't see any ligaments on her, after all.

'Randall!' cried Diane. 'You're the only one who'll believe me!'

'Believe what?' Randall spluttered, feeling a surge of energy despite not getting enough sleep.

'It's Samantha!' Diane said, 'I think she's up to something.'

'Wouldn't surprise me,' growled Randall. 'You see her smile? But what do you think she's up to?'

'She was out and about where she shouldn't be,' said Diane, her face scrunching despite the lack of skin. It reminded Randall of the Humpties. 'Seems odd behaviour for who is supposed to Santa's most loyal servant.' She shuddered. 'I also sensed a touch of necromancy when she appeared.'

'Necromancy?'

'Yes,' she said. 'I've seen souls of Purgatory interested in it before. They believe it can be used to bring them back to life.'

'Really?' Randall immediately grabbed Diane by the shoulders.

'What are you doing?'

'Sorry,' said Randall, regaining himself. 'It's just, at this point, I'd give anything to be alive again. Just to go home and get on with my life and forget all this nonsense. I want my fingers back, you know.' Diane seemed to flinch. 'You okay?'

'You're here for a reason,' said Diane as she got a cigarette from her pocket. 'There's a reason you haven't gone straight to Heaven or Hell. You may not be evil enough, but you're not good enough either.'

'Well,' said Randall, fiddling about with his antlers. 'Can't I be more gooder back home or something?'

Diane slapped him.

A moment of silence followed, with Randall rubbing his nose and Diane narrowing her eyes with eyelids of bone. 'You know,' said Diane, 'You are exactly what's wrong with this realm. A refusal to grow up. Don't get me wrong, I think the fact that they are giving presents to the people of Purgatory is good….but…

'I came here to talk to Santa.' She took out a lighter and lit her cigarette. 'Let him find me. He's had an influence on you, he has.' After taking a drag, she turned back to Randall.

'Diane,' said Randall, 'Don't you ever get tired of your job? Don't you want to be alive again?'

Shaking her head, Diane replied, 'You know, when I was alive, I did things I wasn't proud of, but I had to support my mother. Do you want to know why I'm a skeleton?'

Randall felt a chill. 'Why?'

'I made money…through my body,' replied Diane, hanging her head, burying her face with her hand. 'We were poor', she repeated, 'and we lived in such squalid conditions. I worked and worked, hoping to improve our lives, but we ended up cold…and soon I was here.'

She then talked about how her original duty was as a carpenter, as she had helped one in life, and how she had volunteered for the role of Ghost of Christmas Yet to Come when it had come up. How, after several successful hauntings, she had been offered ascension.

'I couldn't,' she said. 'Not when there were more people like those I had visited. Not when I still had work to do. Not when mum was…'

'What happened to your mum?'

'I think you can figure it out,' said Diane, taking another drag. She was silent for a few more minutes before she looked out of the window. 'Santa should be here by now. Least one of his helpers.'

'You really want them to stop by?' asked Randall.

'If I'm not going to tell him, who will?' She opened Randall's door, sending some of the cigarette smoke outside the door. Randall thought that as long as Diane was here, he might as well make conversation, but what about?

His death? Maybe she still felt responsible. Definitely not *her* death or her mother's death. She didn't like all the *Christmas Carol* movies, so, thought Randall, she'd likely give another slap just for mentioning the *Flintstones* version.

'Your life,' said Diane, 'what was it like?'

Randall froze for a moment – he was worried she might be offended if he talked about being well-off as opposed to what she went through – but then thought, *hey, she asked for it.*

'Well, I'm about 25, or was, rather. I took maths and English at University and got a job as a data entry clerk. I moved out of my mum's a couple years or so ago, and I had a girlfriend but now we just remain…we stayed friends when I was alive, I mean.'

'Okay then,' replied Diane. 'Has anyone ever told you you're a bit awkward?'

'Yes,' sighed Randall, 'Several times.'

'Maybe that's why you're in Purgatory,' replied Diane with a snide smile, 'They thought you would socialise better here.'

'Maybe it is,' replied Randall with a small laugh. 'Wow, you know for someone who teaches people how to be nice, you can be a bit nasty at times.'

'My job is to make people aware of their flaws,' said Diane, 'so they can fix them. You've seen all my movies, you should know that.'

'Yeah, well anyway, shouldn't we be focussing more on Samantha and what she's apparently doing?'

Just as Randall said that, another reindeer burst through the door. Of course, Randall was ready to say 'Speak of the devil' and demand answers, but it wasn't Samantha. It was another reindeer, a male, whose eyes popped when he saw Diane.

'Oh,' said Diane. 'I'm sorry I'm here. I'll go as soon as Randall tells me something he thinks Santa should hear.' Diane winked.

'It's Samantha,' said Randall, waving an arm about. 'We think she's experimenting with necro...evil magic.'

The reindeer nodded, and held both of them by the hands, bringing them to Santa's main building, and up the stairs to Santa's office. Randall half-expected to see a half-asleep Santa in a little nightcap and jammies, but no, there he was behind his desk, wide awake and still wearing his Christmas jumper.

'Diane!' he yelled, almost dropping his cocoa, 'What are you doing here?'

Before Diane could answer, the reindeer who brought her to the office spoke. 'I found her in this reindeer's house. He was saying Samantha was up to something.'

'Yeah,' said Randall. 'I saw her go outside your realm.'

Santa raised an eyebrow. 'How did she get outside?'

'Well, that I can't remember, but I sensed...I felt that she had been experimenting with dark magic.'

'How did you know she had been using necromancy?' said Santa, 'You haven't been dead long enough to be able to sense it. Did Diane tell you?' Randall said nothing. 'Randall, I'm not cross with you. I said, did Diane...'

'Yes,' replied Diane, folding her arms, 'I did. I came here to talk to you.'

'Diane,' said Santa, 'You know you are not welcome here, especially if you are going to influence my reindeer like this.'

'You're not exactly a good influence either,' said Diane. 'I have a new Ghost of Christmas Past, and he's reluctant to do his job, partly because about how you feel about what we do.'

'I daresay he should ask someone to give him a new duty,' said Santa, 'Christmas is not a time to be reminding one of their mistakes, it is a time to forget the bad and remember the good.'

'So, you'd rather just forget all the bad things rather than learn from them? And children see you as some sort of wise teacher?' Diane sounded like a headmistress telling off a rambunctious pupil. 'Still, that does explain a bloody lot, doesn't it?'

'Hey!' said Randall, with both Diane and Santa staring at him. 'What about Samantha?'

'Randall,' said Santa, 'Samantha is my most loyal and trustworthy reindeer, and I hope you follow her example. I know her well enough to know that she would never dabble in necromancy.'

'Okay then,' replied Randall. 'Can I go now then?'

'You may,' replied Santa, 'Just don't let *her -*' he shot Diane the evil eye - 'influence you any further, and certainly don't let her stay in your house.'

'You are utterly unbelievable,' sighed Diane. 'You know, I've seen some of those Christmas specials and those Disney movies you play non-stop. They say to love your enemies, treat others as they wish to be treated. That's what I'm doing now, and that's what I have been doing.'

'Oh really?' said Santa, sounding somewhat hoarse. 'You really believe people enjoy what you do to them? Scaring them stupid with graveyards and goblins?'

'They aren't supposed to enjoy it, you idiot. Self-improvement isn't supposed to be fun. Nothing's all smiles, not even your job.'

'But aren't they miserable enough without you and your friends frightening them? Maybe they'd be nicer were they happier.'

'Some of them are too happy. I think it's good that you give gifts, but some people I haunt, they're the way they are because they've been given too much. Their parents spoiled them silly and they think they're better than everyone else. They need a kick and I'm supplying that kick.'

'And a lot of people are disagreeable as they simply never got what they wanted for Christmas.'

'No, that's just in those cartoons you force your servants to watch. No-one I've visited became the way they are solely because they didn't get an iPod.'

'No-one deserves more misery. No-one deserves to be afraid.'

'You make people afraid. You say, if you're not good, you don't get presents.'

'That's the same with you! The people you change don't really change; they only change due to fear of punishment.'

Diane slammed her fist against the table. 'I made you what you are!'

At that point, both Randall and the other reindeer left.

As he made his way back to his little hovel, one thought repeated itself through Randall's head: *I've got to get out of here.* Didn't Santa say that he could ask for another Purgatory duty? If he could get one out of here, at least then he'd be away from Diane and Santa and Samantha, and maybe he'd be something more humanoid. If he were a skeleton, at least he'd have more fingers.

But even if he did have another job, he'd still be in Purgatory. He'd still be dead. He'd still have the knowledge that his favourite childhood characters were real and didn't like each other. What was here for him in Purgatory? These overly-happy reindeer and elves had nothing to teach him, and he was certain the people outside this place wouldn't be much better.

There was no-one like Mother. No-one like Alice. No-one like Rob or Dick.

So if Samantha knew a way to be brought back from the dead, he knew he would be stupid not to take it. That reindeer had a darn good reason for wanting to be alive! She seemed to be about his age – another one who died too young – and all that smiling and joy she exuded didn't seem natural at all. She was simply playing a part, and resurrection could mean that she could finally be herself.

Though he tried and tried, Randall couldn't find a single redeeming quality about the festive realm. A whole entertainment centre? Just the same old corny Christmas specials he had seen a million times before, without a real TV programme or movie to be found anywhere. Grass tasted good, but that wasn't something he'd really admit. This place did have turkey and mince pies and cocoa but Earth had that too, and it had lots of other foods too. ✂

This whole land was in tribute of the birthday of a man who turned water into wine, and yet, not a drop of alcohol was allowed in these premises. The fact that Diane drank meant beer must exist in Purgatory, so the thought of a simple reassignment did tingle in Randall's brain, but he decided he would prefer real beer, real beer with real friends.

He considered asking for a reassignment, but that would mean a discussion with "Them". Just the thought of "Them" or whatever they were gave Randall a chill down his spine, but part of him wanted to meet with Them just to see if he could punch Them. Punch them for not stopping Diane and Santa's little spats, for letting Santa's realm stay as stagnant as it was.

His door was open. Diane was there, scowling. Though she wasn't wearing a robe, she had become the crimson spectre that had terrorised Mr. Magoo.

'Are you thinking about joining in on necromancy?' she asked, 'Don't.'

Then she left.

Chapter 8

He had asked for reassignment, but they refused.

    All it took was a simple request, he was told. Just tell them he wanted asylum from the brats screeching about his work, just tell them he wanted to write stories about things other than Edward the Duck, just tell them to bring him somewhere in Purgatory other than Toyland.

    As soon as he thought of it, he announced his plans to other Toylanders, and was met with gasps and jeers. The first Humpty he had told scrunched his face into a hideous grimace, making him seem more an ovular rubber gargoyle than an egg. The guilt trip he gave was much less severe than what he received in Hell, but it still rang in his brain. Not in a way that made him want to recant, but in a way that made him want to hit himself in order to force the memory out of his head.

    'Don't you want to stay here?' said the Humpty, 'Don't you know what these children have died of? You are part of a system that brings these children comfort and joy, which they are in dire need of after what they have been through. I once met a little boy who died of a terrible illness, and he told me he loves your *Edward* books because Edward reminds him of his dad who he hopes to reunite with in Heaven one day.' Barnaby had heard souls that had ascended communicated with the people of Purgatory from time to time, especially family members, yet he hadn't heard anything from his parents or any of his other relatives.

Though Barnaby didn't wish to go back to Hell, the image of that boy ending up there made him smirk.

He asked them for a reassignment – *them* this was – and they point blank refused. They would give reassignments to janitors or postmen or drivers, they said, but Barnaby's job was too precious. He was given a special role for the little kiddies to make them happy. What made children so special? Because Jesus told his followers to be like the little children? But did not the Bible also say to put away childish things? Edward wasn't supposed to be childish, but everyone had made him out to be, so he had to be put away.

Santa was childish, too.

So no reassignment for Barnaby then. And his attempts to be wed to Mary ended in disaster, too. Though that was because he didn't plan enough.

This was planned out though. Planned by Samantha and Derek and Carl, with a little help from himself. Cages fashioned for supernatural beings so they wouldn't do any more trouble. For Santa and the Christmas ghosts and the reindeer who refused. With his little knowledge of hellfire and Purgatory, Barnaby knew which spells and magic would be the most effective. Some of the supernatural power of the forces of Hell must have rubbed off on him.

And it would grow on Christmas Eve too.

'Hey, Barnaby,' said Carl. 'Try them out now.' Barnaby looked at the spell, read the words aloud, and cages made of spectral energy appeared, white blazing sparks of light forming bars.

'Marvel,' said Barnaby, 'A true marvel.'

'Well,' laughed Derek, 'we pleased Mr. Unpleasable, we must be doing something right.'

'Of course,' said Barnaby, pointing to the ceiling, 'we still have to make sure we can bring our intended prey here.'

'Leave that to Samantha.' Carl and Derek both nodded.

Randall had had his first dream since he came here. Most of his sleeps here had been uneasy and blank, but he had actually had a dream, and so close to Christmas too. Like most dreams he had, he had forgotten most of it, but there were images that stuck with him.

He was certain he saw his father.

Though it was the bell clanging that got him out of bed, Randall didn't truly awaken until Samantha burst through the door, looking not too dissimilar from Diane when she did the same. No, she was worse than Diane – she did that smile.

'Come on, lazy bones!' she said, jogging on the spot. 'The big day's coming soon, and you have to get fit!' Oh joy. More trophies.

'You!' said Randall. 'I was told that –'

'You don't believe that, do you?' said Samantha, seriously looking as if she were about to cry. Yes, it actually looked genuine. Randall had seen a million kids with that expression; must be a side-effect of working here. After those big doe eyes, however, there followed that scowl. 'Not from that heartless skeleton.'

'Yeah,' said Randall, 'I think there's something up with her too.'

'I'm glad you think so,' said Samantha, 'Santa's really worried about you, and, well, I'm worried about you too.' She put her hooves on his shoulders. 'Have you visited your fath…your family?'

All of a sudden, what happened last night faded away. A – slightly odd- rush of comfort filled Randall, that made him simultaneously feel like lying down and feel like going onto the track again.

'Look,' she said. She did sound like Alice. 'After training today, why not see your family and friends again? Santa told me he thinks you should.' Randall said nothing. 'Look, Santa doesn't decide who ascends or descends; you have no reason to be afraid of him. And the fact that you haven't descended yet must mean you're doing something right here. Now, let's go to training.'

Alice. She was the reindeer equivalent of Alice. Alice back in the old days too. When they went to the cinema together, when they sat in the park and just looked up at the sky, saying nothing. Those memories were what kept him through the year just as much as Christmas, even if they carried a tiny little sting. For so long he had wished for Alice back, and now he had that feeling he had with her again, sprouting inside of him.

So off he went onto the racetrack for some training for the big night. He did much better than he usually did, making record time and not even tripping once. The trophy he got was the same trophy everyone else got though. Then there was weight-lifting, treadmills, and even a bit of Blind Man's Bluff. Santa said it was to help build relationships and to build stronger navigation skills, but Randall found himself hopeless at it, given he couldn't remember half of the reindeer's names.

What followed was lunch: turkey with gravy and mashed potatoes, mince pies for pudding and a cup of hot chocolate. More training followed afterwards, with congratulations given by all. 'You did brilliantly, Randall!' 'Good job!'

Though Randall did think he could use some encouragement here and there to prepare him for what he was about to do, the silence of his home calmed him as opposed to the uproar in the racetrack. So all he had to do was focus on his childhood home and he would temporarily appear there, though no-one would apparently see him.

It wasn't long until Christmas Eve, and Randall was certain he had been told that you slowly gain the power given to you by Christmas. He could make Mum catch a brief glimpse of him, or at least give her the idea that he was okay.

Randall attempted to picture his mother's bright smile, the one she gave when she opened her presents, but found it replaced with Diane's undead scowl. It was Samantha that said he should visit his family, and that angry skull told him not to listen to Samantha. Samantha was up to something, the skull said, so maybe Randall going to Earth was part of her plan.

But Alice though.

Samantha was a sign. How she sounded and acted was a sign that Randall needed to see her again. He couldn't refuse an opportunity like this out of something like paranoia.

Scrunching up his eyes, Randall thought of home.

'Okay,' said Diane, holding a bunch of papers. 'We still got a couple of days. Let's go over it.' Diane almost felt like she should have been wearing a beret and puffy trousers with boots – she was sitting in a lawn chair after all, which was sort of like a director's chair.

Marcus stood, shimmering with an ethereal glow provided by Paul, donning a silver business suit. 'I am the Ghost of Christmas Past.'

'Too soft,' replied Diane. 'Sound authoritative. You're like a news reader; people expect you to be formal and serious, not scruffy and soft. Speaking of which, you've got a hair out of place there. Come here.' Diane then walked up to Marcus and smoothed down his hair. 'Just because you're dead doesn't mean you don't have to wash.' After that, she dove back onto her chair. 'Now let's go through that again.'

He just stood there.

'Oh God.' Diane began massaging her temples. 'Just because I smoothed down your hair?'

'No,' replied Marcus, 'It's what you told me about that reindeer. How she had that sense of necromancy.'

'Don't worry about her,' said Diane. 'I've seen other people here try to use necromancy. It always horribly backfires. Once again, when it comes to Santa and his reindeer, it's usually me they're after. You're new; I've been here from the start.'

'That doesn't mean they won't try and get me, too.'

'Don't worry,' Diane repeated, though looking somewhat antsy herself. 'I'll protect you. Now again, with more authority.'

Marcus stood firm, resembling a judge about to pass sentence. 'I am the Ghost of Christmas Past.'

'Much better,' Diane said with a smile. 'Let's do the whole thing.'

For all of the criticism Diane gave Marcus, he actually did take the time to learn his script by heart, and recited every word Diane had written down for him. A shame that he seemed to have learnt it too well.

'No, no, you sound too monotonous. And didn't I tell you to ad-lib? Add accusations and comments to make it seem more genuine?'

'I just couldn't think of any,' replied Marcus. 'Maybe I'll think of some when the actual night comes?'

'Oh brother,' said Diane, laughing slightly, 'You really are hopeless, aren't you? Now, let's go through…wait.' Diane stood up, looking around and sniffing like she was a dog.

'What are you doing?'

'Marcus, get out of here.'

'I wasn't that bad, was I?'

'No, seriously. Get out. Run for your…just run!'

Shrugging, Marcus ran out of Diane's house as Diane neared the window, a fierce expression on her skull. 'I know you're out there,' she said. 'Come on out.'

'Poor Diane,' said a voice. 'I know you're frustrated. I know you're underappreciated. What if I told you I could change all that?'

Folding her arms, Diane continued to stare out of the window. 'I know what you're going to ask me and the answer is no. Don't you know how long I've been doing this job, and how many times people have offered me resurrection? I don't want it. I still have work to do. And don't you know how dangerous this stuff is?' She slammed her fist on the windowsill. 'You'll die again, you know. You'll descend instantly afterwards.'

'Does that really matter? Barnaby escaped Hell; I'm sure someone as smart as you could as well.'

'You are implying I would want to do that?'

'But don't you want some flesh on those bones again? Don't you want to be beautiful? Loved?' That last word was said in a venomous tone. 'If you stay in Purgatory, you will continue to be reviled by Santa and his followers; you will continue to be feared rather than beloved. If you let yourself be resurrected, I can help you make some new friends, I can make things better for you.'

'I'm needed.'

'No you're not. You said it yourself, people ignore you, overlook you. And did you see how apathetic that Ghost of Christmas Past was? You're going to get more like him, you know. If you join me, you could forget all this. You could be happy.'

'No, no, no.'

'Very well,' replied the voice, 'I suppose that doesn't really matter.'

Diane was seized by her wrist.

So here he was, back home. Randall had thought about going back to his flat, but it'd have likely been cleaned out by now. No, he was back where he was supposed to be. It was usually around this time he'd leave his flat and visit Mum for the holidays. He'd come with a big bag of presents, and sometimes he'd even make mince pies or cookies for her.

Oh God, thought Randall, *Santa really did rub off on me*.

When Randall arrived here, he half-expected to see the house completely bare, but instead was glad to see that the tinsel, the garlands and the Christmas tree were still up. Dad wanted them to still put up Christmas decorations as he lay dying, and Randall wanted the same. The TV was on, with *Homeland* playing, yet Mum couldn't be seen on the sofa. Randall tried sitting on the sofa, just to see if he could actually sit down as opposed to just falling through, and yes, he could sit down.

Jacob Marley could sit down.

As soon as he sat down, Mum entered the room with a glass of water, and she sat down right beside Randall. *She didn't sit on top of me*, Randall thought, *so maybe she does sense me, perhaps? Perhaps?*

'Mum,' said Randall, tapping his mother on the shoulder. No, not tapping, his hoof went right through her. 'Mum, it's me, Randall. Can you hear me? Can you sense me?' When Mum put the water down, Randall reached for it. He had seen ghosts in the movies make stuff float, and he had been living in a movie for the past few days, so why not?

Nope, his hoof went through the glass, though he still felt a bit of the cool water. For a minute, it felt like his fur was wet, but it was completely dry. His Mum continued to stare blankly at the TV screen in silence. 'Mum!' Randall said again, to no response.

Well, if he used his mind to get here, maybe he could use his mind to make his Mum know that he was here. He stared at the glass of water with wide, unblinking eyes, filling his brain with commands to make the glass float.

Glass float.
Glass float glass float alice alice
No, concentrate on the glass diane is mad glass float glass santa float
Alice Samantha diane santa
Glass glass glass glass

The glass toppled over.

Well, that was something. Wasn't much, but it was something. All that came out of it was Mum turning to the glass and walking to the kitchen to get a kitchen towel. What else did the ghosts do in the movies? They wrote messages, didn't they? A pencil, a piece of paper, anything.

Randall got off of the seat and into the kitchen. Ah, yes, Mum always kept a shopping list on the fridge with a pen handy. When Randall tried to pick up the pen, he went right through it again. So concentrate again. Float pen, he thought, float pen.

The pen actually began to levitate.

Now write, "I'm here, Mum."

The pen fell down.

Randall couldn't help but yell, 'Damn it!' and that is when he saw his Mum turn around, just to turn back again. *Okay, let's try that.* 'Mum!' he cried like a kid wanting to go to the sweet shop. 'Mum! It's Randall! *Randall!*'

At that point, the pen floated up and wrote "Randall" on the pad. *Oh, well look at that.* Mum turned around and approached the fridge. She took a look at the pad and the writing on it. 'Mum!' cried Randall again, jumping up and down and waving his arms around. 'Mum, I'm here!'

She took a look at the pad, gave a quizzical look, and then threw the note in the rubbish.

Oh well. Shrugging, Randall followed his mother back into the living room and sat beside her as she watched *Homeland.* Even if she couldn't see him or was denying his existence, he at least could watch TV with her again. If she knew he was there, she'd let him watch with her, no matter what species he was or whatever he could make pens do.

The programme ended, and Randall almost instantly returned to his home in Purgatory, though he wasn't sure whether it was him that did it or it was some time limit. Did Santa bring him back? If so, would Santa really let him watch *Homeland*? That didn't seem like the type of show Santa would approve of.

Still, he wondered if he could try one more. Alice. He'd think of her flat, which he had such fond memories of visiting, and see if he'd have better luck managing to get her to sense him. Maybe Lenny would be there too. After the type of things Randall had seen and learned in Purgatory, hearing Lenny bug him would be a blessing. At least Lenny was actually predictable.

In his mind's eye, he had a perfectly formed picture of Alice's flat. Light grey walls, red curtains, potted plants and wooden sculptures of cats. And the TV where they sat together and laughed at cheesy old movies on the science fiction channel.

All he had to do was think really hard, and what he wanted would appear right before him. He wouldn't get back together with Alice, but at least he'd see her again. So he shut his eyes and tried to imagine the cool breeze from her window, the sounds of cars passing by, the scent of the cinnamon she liked to cook with.

When he started to feel himself dematerialising, he was greeted not by the smell of cinnamon or of Alice's scented candles, but rather the smell of meat. Was Alice cooking something then? An early Christmas dinner? No, it wasn't meat, it had that same hot and cold feel as the air of Santa's realm. He felt harsh heat against his fur, and yet he also felt soothing snow.

Upon opening his eyes, Randall found himself not in Alice's flat, but staring instead at a picture of some arcane symbol, with a myriad of writing he couldn't read. Turning around, he saw a whole bookshelf haphazardly stuffed with dusty old tomes. Atop it were a framed picture of an old lady and a bobblehead of Brian from *Family Guy*. Where was he?

'Randall! It's you!' Randall swerved away from the bookshelf and looked behind him to see none other than Diane, trapped behind bars that looked like frozen candy floss. In front of the cage stood an old man in a porkpie hat and a tweed jacket, drumming his fingers over a cane. Beside him was a circular table with a pyramid atop it, glowing. 'I know you're here, Mr. Reindeer,' said the old man. 'Why don't you try and talk to me?'

Randall quivered, and found himself with the urge to throw something at this smirking man. The only thing keeping him from taking a book and chucking it was the fact that he was physically unable to do so, This man was what reeked of the burning chilling meat, as if his very flesh was cooking. There was also a sense of déjà vu in the air...*this is going to be another Christmas character*, thought Randall, *I just know it.*

'You don't seem to be much for conversation,' said the old man, 'So I suppose I'll be doing the talking. My name is Barnaby; you may remember me from Toyland.'

Think about Purgatory think about Purgatory

'Oh, are you trying to leave? Awfully impolite of you, I must say. Fortunately, there's a teeny bit of magic in the air that prevents you from leaving, at least for a little while. You're the newest of Santa's recruits, aren't you?'

Randall would have nodded, but then he remembered Barnaby probably didn't see him, so he said 'Yes.' It sounded like a snake's hiss.

'Well, you may have heard that I was like you. I was dead and forced into a position I didn't want to be in. But look at me now; flesh and blood again.'

Diane stood up and violently threw herself against the candy floss bars that now imprisoned her. 'Don't listen to him! Run!'

'Quiet you,' said Barnaby. 'On Christmas Eve, the powers of the supernatural world will be at their fullest, and this is when we can cast a resurrection spell on the recently-deceased. The problem is, it only works if the client is willing to cooperate.' Barnaby hung his head and sighed. 'I have so longed to bring life back to poor Diane here — the girl deserves it — but she is too stubborn to go along. She seems to believe she's perfectly content being a bag of bones.'

Diane's eyes seemed to burn red. 'Go to Hell.'

Book float. Book float. Then book throw. Book float book throw. Book float throw.

A book plopped down from the shelf.

Now throw. Now throw.

'Listen,' snarled Barnaby, revealing his yellowed picket fence teeth, 'I know you hate being in that nicey-nice pit Santa calls a realm. Don't think "they" are going to give you a new task either. I may be your only exit. Your life was cut short, and I only wish to remedy that.' He gestured towards Diane, who was still scowling. 'Do you want to be like her, Randall? Her life was stolen from her, she was kidnapped by Purgatory, and now she has Stockholm Syndrome. Do you want to continue being caught between afterlives until you're no longer relevant?'

Randall didn't respond. He thought about trying the book again, but his mind seemed to have shut down. All that seemed to exist was him, Barnaby and Diane's glare.

'You're seriously considering it, aren't you?' said Diane. 'You idiot.'

'Just think how happy your friends and family would be. Just think how happy you would be. You could accomplish more than you could ever hope to accomplish at that pseudo-North Pole. You could get married and have children. Better still, Santa won't have the opportunity to brainwash you into a mindlessly happy clone of himself.'

'You'll still die,' growled Diane, 'and you'll go straight to Hell afterwards!'

'Ooh,' said Barnaby, taking a look at his watch. 'We're out of time. You can go back to Purgatory now, maybe sleep on what I've told you. I'm certain we'll meet again.'

Randall found himself running towards Barnaby and Diane, hoof-hands balled into fists. Despite what he knew, he tried to hit Barnaby right in the face, only to hit one of Diane's bars. What felt like a hundred volts ran through Randall's body. Though he no longer had any insides, he felt them being fried.

For a second, everything went black, and then he was back in his home sweet home in Purgatory, lying on the floor. Samantha was there.

'Are you okay?' she said, smiling her infamous smile. 'Did you have fun visiting your family?'

'You...' croaked Randall, trying to force himself off of the floor. 'You're working with Barnaby, aren't you?'

'Barnaby?' she said, laughing. 'That old blowhard? Why would I work with a big meanie like him?'

'I know you are...I know...and what have you done with Diane?'

That smile of hers turned into a smirk. 'Yes, yes, I am working with him. What are you going to do about it? Tell Santa? He's not going to believe you. "That dern Ghost of Christmas Yet to Come ruined his brain," that's what he'll say.'

Randall got up off of the floor, and looked at Samantha straight in the eyes. 'Can you lot really bring me back to life?'

'Of course we can,' replied Samantha. 'If you really want it.'

'I-I do,' blurted out Randall, 'I want to be alive.'

'Well, you'll have to wait until Christmas Eve then,' said Samantha, stroking Randall's fur. 'There's some sort of time limit on these things. Since you've been dead for less than a month, Christmas Eve is the only time you can get resurrected. Barnaby could have it before then because he's been dead a long time, so could Diane.'

'I want away from them,' said Randall. 'Away from Santa and Diane. You know what? Forget I asked what you did with Diane. I'm glad you dealt with her.'

'Me too,' said Samantha. 'They're both as bad as each other they are, both of them. Both of them brainwashing people to think like they do. And to think, we used to watch all their movies and believe their messages.'

All doubts evaporated from Randall's gut, and he let Samantha run her hooves through his fur. 'Yeah,' he said. 'Definitely.'

Samantha held Randall by the shoulders and stared into his eyes. 'Come on, Randall, join me. A lot of other reindeer are. Just think of what a Merry Christmas it'll be. Everyone being reunited with their families, forever, as humans!' She then smiled, not that fake smile, but a more soothing one. 'I wonder what you look like as a human? I bet you'd look pretty fit.'

Randall laughed, before adding, 'I thought you said…'

'When we're alive again,' said Samantha, 'That won't matter. Nothing about this place will matter. We'll be free.' She held Randall by the forearms. Randall held her by the back. She nuzzled him by the neck and whispered 'Free' one more time.

They kissed.

They held each other and kissed.

All of a sudden, Randall felt like what he was supposed to be. He felt like he was no longer weighed down, like he could soar through the night sky.

'Okay then,' said Samantha as she pulled her snout away from Randall's. 'It's just a matter of time now. We'll both be free soon. And then…' She smiled the soothing smile again before walking out of the house, with Randall watching her leave.

As he watched her, she blew him another kiss. After that, he saw an elf walk by. 'Ah, young love,' he said.

Chapter 9

It wasn't Christmas Eve yet. *The cage can't be that strong.*

Diane had mastered teleportation, and did it quicker and with more clarity than most other spirits. This cage could hold a weaker ghost, but it couldn't hold her. It couldn't hold the Ghost of Christmas Yet to Come.

The image in her mind was clear. Her bungalow, with its TV, its fridge with its six-pack of Carling waiting for her, its chair which she liked to lounge about in. All she had to do was think of it hard enough, and she'd be there lickety-split. As soon as the Carling entered her mind, she already felt her form become gauzier.

Suddenly, she felt a shock.

'You hear that, Carl?' Diane heard Derek say. 'She's trying to magic herself away. Fat chance.'

Diane opened her eyes to see Carl and Derek sitting around the pyramid, enjoying some wine. What she wouldn't give for a drop of the stuff right now.

'Okay,' she said, 'your cage is stronger than I thought. I'll give you that. I wonder why you haven't tried to capture Santa yet.'

'Don't flatter yourself,' said Carl, laughing. 'He's more powerful than you so we need more powerful magic, see?'

'And you can't get it until Christmas Eve,' sighed Diane. 'You know, I do get the feeling that you haven't really planned ahead.'

Derek put down his wine. 'What are you getting at?'

'You know for a fact that Heaven and Hell exist,' said Diane, forming a pyramid with her fingers. 'So if I were you, I'd start making preparations for my passing. I mean, if you don't feel like trying to get into Heaven, you could always practice for Purgatory duty.'

'You know what?' said Carl, holding up a book. 'I think I liked you better when you didn't talk.'

'You can't live forever,' Diane laughed. 'You're going to die one day and you've pretty much punched your ticket to Hell.'

'Oh, that place? I've been there, you know. There and back.' Carl, Diane and Derek all turned around to see Barnaby standing triumphantly in the doorway, raising his cane like a wizard would raise a staff. 'Do you all know what tomorrow is?'

The room was silent.

'This is Christmas Eve Eve, of course!' He looked in Diane's direction. 'Maybe we should have a little party. I mean, Diane, this is pretty much a holiday for you! Are you happy?'

Diane, true to what she was supposed to be, said nothing.

'I know what you're thinking. It was a waste of time resurrecting me because I'll just die again. Well, maybe I'll just get out of Hell again! Really, it's like I'm talking to a child! I won't tidy my room; it'll just get messy again! And besides, even if these souls did go to Hell, wouldn't it be worth it if they had just one more day alive again after suffering through Purgatory? You know, now that I think about it, I've seen things there that make Hell almost pleasant.'

'You spent almost all of your time in Toyland.'

'Exactly!' replied Barnaby, making his phlegm buildup all the more obvious. 'You try spending ten minutes there, let alone years!'

'Hey, Barnaby,' said Derek, 'Come over here and join us for a bit of wine, why don't you?'

'Certainly,' said Barnaby, giving a little bow. 'And why don't we let our guest of honour have a bit too?' He picked up a wine bottle, and threw it at Diane's cage, which missed her. At that, he laughed, which sounded like a duck being strangled. 'Look at you,' said Barnaby, staring at the bars of Diane's cage. 'You're supposed to be some sort of big cheese where you come from, but now, you're just nothing. You really should have taken Samantha's offer.'

'So you've got me,' said Diane. 'And you're going to get Santa. Then what?'

'We'll show people how feeble and meaningless the holiday really is,' replied Barnaby. 'To show how weak its symbols really are.'

'Samantha was just mocking me about how everyone dismisses me as a figment of their imagination. How do you know if you parade me about, people won't dismiss me as a special effect? If you do the same for Santa, how will people know he's not some bloke in a suit?'

'Oh,' said Barnaby, 'We'll make them see. Oh, and that reminds me, Carl, Derek, have you finished our little float?'

'It's coming along.'

'See, you do have some purpose after all. Have you also prepared the extra cages?'

'Yep!'

'Okay then, very good,' said Barnaby, rubbing his hands together. 'I'll get us some more wine. Maybe we can even have some music, too.'

One more day to go.

Randall remembered all the Christmas Eve Eves of his past, when he would gleefully gobble the little chocolate from his little Advent Calendar, prematurely hang up his stocking "just to get it out of the way" until Mum told him no, and in adulthood, he would build up to the bigger Christmas movies in his collection. *Rudolph. It's A Wonderful Life.* Those sorts of movies.

Now that Christmas Eve Eve was here, Randall could still sense some of that excitement, but he also felt quite a bit of dread slinking about. Unlike most December 23rds he had lived through, this date promised something special the very next day, as opposed to the day after next. He would finally leave this shabby, fur-coated body, shed his antlers and hooves and be a living, breathing human again. No more cheesy Christmas movies. No more mince pies and grass.

Still, there was a little poke in his stomach at all this, and he had no idea why there was. The very second he came here, he wanted to be human again, and now he had that chance. He was an animal now, and he was pretty certain all animals wanted to be human. It would explain why his old dog was always trying to get up onto seats.

A reindeer burst into Randall's little house. Randall shrieked a bit, thinking it was Samantha, but no, it was Billy. Billy, the reindeer who always went onto the racetrack panting and wheezing, and yet always getting a little trophy to take home. 'Come on,' said Billy, looking and sounding more like a pig than a reindeer. 'Last day of training.' Randall followed him.

'Billy,' said Randall, 'Did Samantha – did she…'

'Oh, her?' said Billy, with Randall feeling some more dread climbing out of his stomach. That dread subsided somewhat as Billy smiled. 'You're in love with her, aren't you? Didn't you two share a kiss? She never talks to me, she does.'

'Yeah,' said Randall, laughing half because of Billy and half to ease the dread. 'We had a kiss.'

'Okay,' giggled Billy, 'But enough about that. Let's go!' Just then, he took to the air and flew off.

Randall stood in the moment, standing dumbfounded. He didn't have to wait until the next day. He could fly if he wanted to.

Taking his forelegs out of the snow, he raised them into pseudo-aeroplane position. 'Neee-ow!' he said, even if he felt embarrassed while doing so. 'Lift off!' He ran down the snow towards the racetrack, and sure enough, he took flight.

The wind blew fiercer and wilder than it ever had before, and Randall embraced it as he pierced it, and burst through the skies. The purple sky which for so long had seemed so artificial and stale was now suddenly filled with life. Clouds he had never seen before surrounded them, and were so close Randall felt he could touch them, mould them, cling onto them. At last, he finally felt like this was a real place.

He finally felt like he could do the duty he was given.

He swam through the sky – it did indeed feel like swimming through cool, cleansing waters – and before his eyes, he saw another gauzy reindeer doing the same. Then he felt the weight of a sleigh behind him, and heard a familiar laugh. Then there was the thought of sad souls, attempting to get into Heaven, receiving presents that would boost their morale. He would drop down onto roofs, people would get the same tingle of excitement they felt as a child, and next morning, they would have a reminder that there was still the chance of ascension.

Though Randall did imagine how someone would react if they wanted a DVD of *The Royle Family*, and instead received a DVD of *Rainbow*. If they wanted Guinness and received root beer.

Well, that wouldn't happen this year, would it? Most of the reindeer would be human again, and Santa would be trapped in that candy floss cage, never to deliver presents not just for this year, but for every year following. If that cage was strong enough to hold the mighty Ghost of Christmas Yet to Come, it could hold the very embodiment of Christmas spirit. Santa would be trapped while his servants – and Randall – would be enjoying being reborn.

Just then, another reindeer, a real one, flew up to Randall. 'OK,

I know you're enjoying yourself, but could you please come down?'

'Sorry,' said Randall, and he dove down onto the race track where the other reindeer were, including none other than Samantha. She was standing on her hind legs, yet still floating, and all the other reindeer were looking in her direction. A clanging from the elf's bell, and she reverted to all fours.

'Okay,' said the elf. 'We may not be at full power yet, but you can still fly, so let's practice that. Hey, Randall! I just saw you.' Randall froze. 'You were doing great up there, considering it was your first time! Here!' Guess what? It was another trophy. ✗

He joined the racetrack, floating above it. What followed was a race, which was just slightly above the ground so Randall didn't feel the freedom of the sky. It reminded Randall of that one time he went go-carting with his housemate from university. Samantha was the winner, and when she passed the finish line, every reindeer clapped. They all received prizes, and because it was the day before Christmas Eve, they were special ones. Teddy bears.

Randall took a brief look at his teddy. Fat lump with a little green bowtie. Randall had no real memories involving teddy bears. They never helped him sleep – if they did, they weren't as effective as the books he was forced to study in school – they never fought off any monsters, and he didn't remember assigning any of them any significance. The only teddy-related memory he could think of was when he and Dick were at Rob's house and watched *Ted* drunk.

Still, he took the teddy bear – he didn't bother giving it a name – and brought it back to his house, resting it on the bed. Straight after doing this, he wondered why he bothered being so careful with the bear, considering he would be leaving soon. Leaving to where Diane was caged…but she deserved that, didn't she? Both she and Santa deserved it for their brainwashing and their childish arguments. He had it coming by making everything all nicey-nice and she had it coming for giving him so many nightmares as a kid.

Did I just think that?

He then returned for more training, and his last lunch. His last meal. *If – no, when – I get resurrected,* thought Randall, *I'll never touch another mince pie again.* In fact, he would drink more alcohol than ever, just to spite Santa. Without the ghosts of Christmas to nag him either, he could live however he wanted…

Before going to Hell.

As he sat down to lunch – an extra big one as Santa thought

the reindeers could use some extra strength, though Randall didn't know what sort of strength eggnog brought – Randall thought back to when Diane scowled at him, warned him. Well, that was her job, wasn't it? The very job she refused ascension for. It was the general selfishness of some people – People like Samantha? People like him? – that made her carry on.

He shrunk into his seat, until Samantha herself came up to him. 'Hey,' she said, with that terrible smile again, 'What's the matter?'

Something wriggled inside Randall. Something squirmed –no, it shook and screamed and wailed and beat at its bars. It was caged like Diane, like Santa and a lot of these other workers would be. He had to yell it. He had to yell everything about Barnaby and the spells and Diane and everything.

It rose from the pits of his stomach, growing more and more as it did, inflating to Herculean proportions…

'I said, what's the matter?'

Whatever it was, it sank all the way back down. Randall's throat had turned to rubber.

'Nothing,' he squeaked out.

'Maybe you should go back home and have a rest, and sit out the rest of the training. I'm sure Santa wouldn't mind.'

'OK,' replied Randall, staggering away from the cafeteria and towards his house, back where'd he be safe…no, he wouldn't be safe. Samantha got in, a skeleton got in, who knows what else might get in? If Barnaby was still on this plane, he could easily get in, as old and crooked as he was. The pictures on the walls now made the house as cold and lonely as the places they depicted, and the bed, with a duvet all red and gold, now had the shadows necessary for monsters to lurk underneath it. The very walls seemed to stretch like that haunted house in Disneyland, making everything all the more lonely and making the shadows all that larger.

He crawled into bed, and held his teddy bear tightly.

Chapter 10

It was now December 24th, and it wasn't just the beeping of her watch that was telling her that. Diane could feel her true power surging through her bones, bringing her enough energy to try and break through the bars again. She dove for them, trying to walk right through them as her kind would a regular wall. Yes, though her eyes were closed, she could feel her palm go through the bars.

Then she heard the voices of Carl and Derek, reciting spells to make the cage stronger. Words spoken with more determination and force than she thought they would have.

This only inspired her to push harder and finally break through the bars, right into reality.

'What?' sneered Carl, 'Get back in there.'

'You think that's going to make me go back in?' Diane said, putting her hands on her hips. 'Now that I'm free, I can do what I'm supposed to do tonight.' She clicked her fingers. Over her grey dress and tights there appeared the traditional black robe and cowl, covering her whole form – in fact, making it as gangly and crooked at that of Barnaby – and bringing forth a torrent of grey smoke.

'We've seen scarier stuff than that in our fridge,' sneered Carl.

'You said it yourself,' said Derek, plumping himself down on a nearby seat. 'In our trade, we see stuff worse than that every day.'

Diane said nothing, and stretched out her skeleton hand.

'Yeah,' said Derek, 'You can cut that out. We know what you

are, there's no need to act.'

At that, Diane instantly pulled down her cowl, just so the two could see her roll her eyes. 'Very well,' she replied, 'but don't you want to see your future? You have a plan, so don't you want to see how it plays out? It would be quite wise.'

'OK then,' said Derek, tossing his hands up in the air. 'Show us our futures then.'

Diane scrunched up her skull again and tried to focus on the future. Not far into the future, just at the end of that day. It would be a future neither she nor the duo would be able to interact with, but if it made them see reason, it would be worthwhile. Indeed, the seed of the vision was in her undead fingers, and it was beginning to sprout.

Another shock. A shock just like those the bars of her cage gave her only intensified, so it felt like her entire form was disintegrating. She didn't have any insides, but she felt a fierce acid within, corroding her. Another blast and she fell to the floor, smoking emanating from her form.

'Now, madam, what were you just doing?' Diane looked up to see Barnaby, holding a piece of parchment in his hand. 'Now, go ahead, my dear, show us all what is to become of us.'

Diane tried again. She thought of the future, but those thoughts were like water in her brain. No seed sprouted from her fingertips. In fact, she began to feel the way she did when she had a Carling too many, and fell on the floor.

'Interesting spell, that,' said Barnaby, waving about the parchment. 'As soon as a spirit is exhibiting its special power, it puts a block on it for about forty-eight hours. So no haunting for you tonight, my dear. I think I did a good thing, actually. Just think, is that not the thing that has made Santa revile you? Maybe if you took a brief break from that sort of thing, he and his realm would be all the more welcoming.'

In seconds, a book flew right into Barnaby's face, knocking him over backwards into a wall, and papers flew up to obscure Carl and Derek's vision. Diane, despite being in a movement-restricting robe, ran right through the walls out onto the streets.

'Barnaby!' cried Carl, pointing in Diane's direction. 'She's getting away!'

'No matter,' said Barnaby. 'Let her go. She'll be even more of a pariah out there than she was in Purgatory. If you're forgetting, we have more important matters at hand. We'll have some very special guests coming in soon.'

Santa rarely ever slept. It was not because he was a spirit – no, they needed to rest as much as the living – but rather because he wanted to get as much done as possible. On this night, and its succeeding day and succeeding night, he slept even less, to make use of the time when his powers were at their fullest. The ability to not only move quickly, but to inspire others to do the same. Various methods of entering a house he was invited into. A vast variety of knowledge.

He was not only supposed to check lists, but check them twice. From his cabinet, he pulled out a piece of paper that resembled a flimsier version of a red carpet. Everyone currently in Purgatory, and not only what they wanted, but what they needed as well. There were many in this plane that needed nothing more than a bright smile were they to ascend. A couple more skeletons had appeared here in the last year – they needed something especially jolly to avoid them becoming downers. There was also someone in Toyland already beginning to have doubts, and Santa didn't want another Barnaby.

The thoughts flooded his brain, each fighting for dominance. One especially prominent thought was how he got into this job, how Diane got him into this job. It was in this office that she finally revealed herself, when she said, 'I'm glad you're enjoying this job', when she asked him out for dinner.

He knew what happened afterwards, but there were more important things to know at that moment. Who would benefit most from a teddy bear, who would benefit most from cartoons? Santa knew. Who was more worthy of being delivered to first? Santa knew.

What he did not know was why there was a thin shadow in the office with him.

Or maybe he did know why. It was just at the moment he knew exactly what Terrance Bomford would like or what reminded Harold Redditch most about his childhood. The problem with the thoughts once they came into his mind was just how much trouble he had organising them. He racked his brains for any mention of a thin shadow; he had seen stranger things in his office, hadn't he?

The shadow exploded, transforming into what looked like a sickly green octopus, its body and tentacles elongated enough that it almost didn't fit into the room. It opened its mouth – its body had a mouth and nothing else – revealing yellow teeth, stained with black, and a tongue as long and slithering as any of its tentacles. Each of its teeth became a head, a shrieking skull that emitted noises that made Santa fall to the ground.

When he fell on his back, Santa found himself unable to get up. It felt like he was under sleep paralysis, and on the night of the year when he had the most energy, too. At first it seemed the beast was lunging over him, but with the blink of an eye, it was replaced by Samantha.

'Samantha,' he said, 'Thank goodness you're here! Someone has...' She put a hoof over his mouth.

'I know,' she whispered. 'You want to know where that creature came from. Well, all answers will be provided soon.'

Randall had another dream. And he remembered it.

He knew he saw his father in it. Desmond, in all his glory, wearing the suit Randall remembered seeing him so often in. He stood as tall and proud as he did when he was alive, and also had an aura attached to his form.

'Randall,' he said, 'I'm sorry this had to happen to you.'

Randall was certain he asked questions, but those were one of the few elements of the dream he had forgotten.

'I was in the same position as you,' said Dad. 'I was working as one of Santa's reindeer too. And yes,' he added, giggling quietly. 'I did get more trophies than I knew what to do with. I pushed on, though. I carried his sleigh all throughout Purgatory. I ran all the races, even helped making the toys, and then...

'Please, Randall, don't give up. I know you will ascend one day if you continue in your duty. I've seen you in college, in university, and I have been proud of the work you put in. I am also glad you chose to keep my memory alive, but do not worry about me now. Stay with Santa.'

Then he was woken up.

He was forced out of Dreamland and back into Purgatory by Samantha, who looked more genuinely gleeful than usual. 'Wake up, lazy bones,' she said. 'The time has come. You and I are going to be human again.' She thumped him with a hoof. 'Look at these. Aren't they disgusting? Well, soon you'll be waving goodbye to them, and you'll have your actual hands back, too!'

'Okay,' said Randall as he was pulled out of his bed, and he looked at his new teddy for one last time. 'Are any others coming?'

'Of course,' she said, winking, 'But I want you to be the first.

The newest one hates the job the most.' She raised her hand, closed her eyes, and whispered for Randall to do the same. In no time, Randall felt his form become less and less substantial, until he heard the sounds of soft pop music and squeaking chairs.

When he opened his eyes, he was greeted with another cage. Its bars weren't made of candy floss; they were made of what looked like dark brown thorns. Animate thorns that slithered through the air like snakes. Behind these bars was none other than Santa Claus, head bowed in disappointment.

'Santa!' cried Randall. 'What happened?'

'Randall?' Santa raised his head. 'Please, leave.'

Before Randall could say anything more, he heard a harsh cough and turned around to see Barnaby wobbling towards Samantha. 'I can see you, my dear,' he said.

'I know,' she replied. 'Do it.'

All of a sudden, Randall got an urge to punch Samantha right in the face, as if that would free Santa, but the very next syllable that exited Barnaby's mouth sent him flying backwards. A thick beam of light emitted from the ceiling – light that was almost the colour of the bars of Santa's cage – and hit Samantha, making her lift from the ground. Bones formed out of nowhere, mimicking her form almost perfectly, before a complete skeleton was built. Randall came closer, but the light grew all the more intense, sending him back again.

Loud noises invaded Randall's ears; shrieks and squeaks and squirms, with a hoarse scream as its crescendo.

As everything grew silent, Randall opened his eyes. Papers were scattered, a chair was knocked over and Samantha was human. A fairly tall brunette, about his age, wearing a red party dress and high heels.

Shuddering slightly from the experience, Samantha raised her hands in front of her face. She held her left hand up to the ceiling, and traced its outline with her right. A laugh that sounded like a cough escaped her throat, but it grew more frantic as she rubbed her arms, and placed her palm against a wall.

'I'm alive!' she squealed, dancing up to Randall. 'I'm alive!' She reached down to grab Randall by the hoof, only for her arm to go through his.

Randall shook just as much as she did when the transformation was complete, and could do nothing but clutch his stomach as if he were about to vomit.

'Randall!' she said. 'I've done it, now it's your turn!'

'Samantha…' Randall and Samantha turned around to see a forlorn Santa, peering from behind the thorns. 'How could you?'

'Shut up!' she snapped. 'Randall,' she cooed, sitting on a nearby table. 'Come on. Don't you want to be with me?' She stretched out a leg, letting a shoe dangle from her toes, and leaned back. 'Come on, I really want to see you as a human.'

Randall stood up, and made his way towards Barnaby, shaking all the more. 'Stop that!' said Barnaby, 'What, are you trying to impersonate an earthquake? Stand still if you want to be resurrected!' Randall did as he was told, though he found himself taking another glance at Samantha, just to make sure what just happened really happened. As soon as Barnaby started reading, Randall turned back to Barnaby, then looked up at the ceiling again, ready to see that burst of green light.

It didn't come.

Shaking the parchment, Barnaby continued to read, his voice increasingly getting harsher and fiercer until he completed the reading and Randall was still a reindeer. Randall looked around for any beams of light, and felt his body to see if his fur had vanished, but no. Still dead, still a reindeer ghost.

'You idiot,' snarled Barnaby, 'You didn't want it! Samantha said you were happy to have a chance to become human again and yet you don't want it? Most spirits would kill for this chance, and several of them are coming here for it! And yet, here you are, content to be dead. Just like Santa here. Just like Diane.'

Samantha looked around the room. 'Where is she, anyway?'

'She managed to slip away, but don't worry,' said Barnaby, smiling. 'She's out and about as a living pile of bones; she's even more isolated than usual.'

She had the picture of her humble bungalow in her head, and she thought that now that she was out of her cage, thinking about it would accomplish something. No matter how much she scrunched her skull, no matter how hard she thought, she was still stuck on the streets. Though she wasn't going a-haunting, she still had her cowl over her face for that was all she had to disguise her true nature. She didn't want to give anyone heart attacks, so she chose not to reveal herself until she could find some help.

The spells had to be reversed, and she needed humans to do it, but what humans would be willing to do so? What humans would be willing to believe?

Scrambling out of the alleyway she was hiding in, Diane took a look around the streets to see any potential candidates. Though she didn't expect much people out and about, she wrung her fingers in worry when she saw no-one. Robe be darned, she ran down the streets, looking out and about for anyone, *anyone*.

The very first sign of life she ran into was a group of drunks, arms around each other, singing a song Diane couldn't understand. She almost ran right through them, but stopped as they passed. 'Hey, what are you doing?' said one of the drunks.

'It isn't Halloween, you twit!'

Diane thought of pulling down her hood and revealing herself, but she knew it wasn't worth the bother. Instead, she stepped onto the road and let them pass, and continued on her journey. She was sure someone would be frightened by her – an old person with one foot in the grave, a sensitive child – but there were greater things to be afraid of right now.

She found herself among places of commerce, but most of them were closed and would stay that way until about the 27th. The streets were adorned with fairy lights and glowing angels and bright Santas, but they only served to emphasise how barren and grey the surroundings were. The only place there seemed to be any life was, oh gods, a pub.

Well, since there were no other options available.

Diane burst in, cowl up and all, to be greeted with a fair amount of people. One of them was singing 'Wonderful Christmas Time' in front of a karaoke machine, but when Diane came in, all eyes were on her.

'See, Matt,' said the landlord, 'I told you you'd had enough. Now you've gone done and died of alcohol poisoning.'

'Hey!' said Diane, a light turning on in her brain. 'You're Matthew MacNathan, aren't you?'

'What about it?'

Diane snarled. 'I haunted you two years ago. I showed you if you keep coming here more than you spend time with your family, your children will grow up bitter and you would die alone.'

'What are you blabbering about?' said Matthew, adjusting his flat cap. 'And what's with that get-up? You part of some cult?'

At this, Diane rushed towards the karaoke machine and seized the microphone - though she didn't grab it, she levitated it so quickly it looked that way - ignoring the man's 'Hey!'

'Everyone! I am the Ghost of Christmas Yet to Come! Santa Claus is trapped at a medium's! I repeat, Santa is trapped! I need someone to accompany me so I can go to save him!'

'All right,' said the landlord, walking towards Diane. 'I don't know what you think you're playing at…'

'It's true!' Diane blurted into the microphone as she removed her cowl. Her skull, with its eyeballs popping out and its long teeth, in all its glory. When the landlord took a few steps back, and she saw everyone stare, Diane made her robe disappear. Now she was wearing her dress, tights and boots, which revealed her skeletal arms. She even detached one of her arms for good measure.

Everyone went crazy.

A nearby patron picked up his glass and threw it at Diane, only for it to go through her. He ran, as did the landlord and two other patrons. Some stayed, staring at Diane in curiosity, and that included Matthew. Raising what counted as her eyebrow, Diane neared Matthew, taking strides as she did so. 'Well?' she said as she brought her face closer to Matt's.

'I'm…' Matthew's eyes were as wide as Diane's. 'I think I hear my wife calling.' He ran out of the door.

Well, at least that wasn't a complete waste of time.

He wasn't stupid. He knew when he was outmatched, and knew how to react. As soon as the resurrection failed, he flew off. Well, at least he thought he did. Though Randall wasn't sure whether or not he tried to fly away, he knew that Samantha was alive again, and Samantha brought him down to Earth and locked him in the same type of cage Barnaby had locked Diane in. Candy floss that shocked him whenever he touched them. He could no longer fly; not that it would do much good, given how small the cage was.

Another reindeer had come to the medium's. He saw Samantha and cheered. He went up to Barnaby, Barnaby performed the spell, and, as promised, the reindeer gained a human body and walked away to be home with his family for Christmas. Randall cried and pleaded all the while, but both Barnaby and Samantha shot him the evil eye.

When the former reindeer left, Samantha turned to Randall and said, 'Don't complain, Randall,' said Samantha. 'I know you'll regret your refusal. I mean, if you keep on refusing until tomorrow, that'll be it. You'll be stuck in that cage until next year.'

Santa angrily laughed, and hearing him do so made Randall shudder a bit. 'He'd rather stay in this cage then participate in your sordid witchcraft,' said Santa, 'and so would I.'

'Oh, Santa,' Samantha sneered, putting her hands on her hips. 'You're so noble. Being the moral one, wasting your time with pointless generosity.'

'Wasting?'

'If you really did deliver presents to *living* children,' said Samantha, 'that would be something. But do you really think the dead have any use for choo-choos and rocking horses? It's Heaven or life these people want, but I very much doubt you'd be able to give them anything like that, now, would you?'

Samantha began to pace around the room. 'I did have faith in you, Santa, really I did. It was you, I thought, that got me and my brothers everything I wanted. Every year I'd build up my list, and everything I asked for, I received. I mean, after all, my dad was the managing director of Holdform Industries, and he told me he had the power to give you my list in person.

'Then one year, something odd happened. I received only half of the gifts I asked for. I got my Sony Walkman, but I didn't get the new dress. I didn't get the new Barbie. Gary and Douglas didn't get half of what they wanted, either. And it happened again next year. I still had faith in you, Santa. I made my lists longer and longer, but got less and less.

'Then I was told you didn't exist, well, at least not in this plane. It was my Dad who got me less and less every year. I still tried to make merry at Christmas, though.' She gestured towards the party dress she was wearing. 'In fact, I think I died because I made a bit too merry. Then again, I'm almost glad I did die. I did learn a few things in Purgatory.'

Her eyes narrowed. 'Do you know why Dad gave me less and less every year? Diane and her two friends gave him a house call. He gave my presents away!'

'Oh for crying out loud!' Randall rose. 'This is all because you didn't get some bloody presents? Seriously, you spoiled brat?'

'You be quiet,' said Samantha. 'It's not just that. It's because of what he and Diane do, forcing people to be all mushy-wushy and nicey-nice. You should just shut up and deliver presents to people who need them. Like me and my family. We had much less money to play with when Dad pissed it all on the poor. Where were you then? Giving a spinning top to some bloke who'd rather be reunited with his daughter?'

'Oh shut up!' spat Randall. 'You know what? You're no reindeer.' He laughed, his chuckling almost sounding like that of a madman. 'They should call you Annabelle, because you're a cow.'

Santa laughed at Randall's remark, but all Samantha said was, 'I have no idea what you're on about.'

'It's this…oh, never mind.' Randall still laughed.

'What are you laughing about?' said Samantha. 'Just think, your family won't see you as a human again and…' Just then, she was hit in the back of the head and collapsed. Barnaby, weak, elderly old Barnaby, had just hit her on the back of the head.

'Always much more satisfying when you have a physical body,' said Barnaby. 'Carl! Derek!' The two popped out from the other room. 'Take her to one of the more orthodox cages.'

'Hold it,' said Derek, 'Don't you owe this girl, isn't she the reason you're here?'

'She helped resurrect me,' said Barnaby, 'I helped resurrect her. As far as I'm concerned, our debt is repaid in full. She brought me here to humiliate Santa, and that is just what I intend to do. A shame that she has to be as bad as he is.'

The three then descended downstairs, leaving Randall alone with Santa. 'Well,' said Randall, attempting to get through the bars again, only to receive another shock. 'This is a situation.'

'It is,' said Santa, still lying on the floor.

'Still, in those Christmas specials you keep showing,' said Randall, though a sting in his tongue told him not to, 'you've faced much worse than this.'

Santa sighed. 'Well, those are just television. Maybe Diane was right.' He buried his face in his hand. 'No, no, I don't know.'

'What do you have against her, anyway?'

'Against? What do I have against her? That sounds a little too harsh. I'm not harsh, am I?'

'It's just,' said Randall, collapsing onto the ground, 'she said something about how she made…'

'She told you, didn't she?' Santa stood up. 'She told you about how she was offered ascension and refused it so she could continue that little job of hers?'

'Oh,' said Randall, 'she said…'

'I can't refuse it if I was never offered it!' snapped Santa, almost pressing his face against the thorny bars. 'I lied about refusing it. They need me.' None of that marshmallow softness his voice had could be found. 'Anyone can be the Ghost of Christmas Yet to Come. They just wear a robe, hide their face and say nothing. There's no reason for Diane to continue on doing her job, but...' He hung his head. 'There can only be one Santa Claus.

'I suppose I should thank Diane, really. It was her and her two friends that got me into this. I used to not care about anyone, but they showed me the light. Once, I only spent my wealth on myself, but after they showed me how I had isolated myself, I would buy toys for children who needed them. They said they were proud of what I did, but my past misdeeds meant I couldn't go to Heaven straight away, and they needed someone in Purgatory to keep the residents' spirits up. I was one of the few in Purgatory to be given my own realm.'

'Finally,' came a small voice. 'Some credit.' Through a wall, there stepped out Diane, wearing her customary black robe. 'You rarely admit that, do you? Ask someone about me, and you always say that I'm just a scary skeleton, I'm just a monster that has no place in jolly Christmas.' She put her skull closer to the bars of the cage. 'You never talk about how I helped you. Or when we were alive, and you saw me on the streets...'

'Diane!' snorted Randall.

'Sorry,' whispered Diane. 'I'm going to save you, but I might need your help, Santa. On this night, you're supposed to know everything about everyone! Tell me someone who can get us out of this mess, or at least willing to read a spell.'

'It's the people of Purgatory I know about,' whispered Santa, 'You should have known that. You also should have known not to come here.'

'Okay,' said Diane, 'Maybe I'll leave you in that cage. You don't seem to enjoy your job anymore anyway. I mean...'

'Careful, careful!' Diane swerved around when she heard Barnaby's voice from the other room. 'We want to keep her alive!'

'Randall!' Diane quietly barked, 'Don't you know anyone who can help? I might know where they are from previous hauntings and visits...like, I think I know where your ex is!'

'No!' Randall almost shouted. 'You keep Alice out of this!'

'I was at the festival she was at,' said Diane, 'and I was there when...'

Just then, Barnaby's steps got louder, and Diane dove through the wall, back onto the streets. Randall felt more dread than ever, imagining Alice's face when a living skeleton came into her house.

Barnaby, Carl and Derek entered, each of them helping to carry Samantha's cage. 'Set it down!' cried Barnaby, and the three did just that, putting her right next to Randall's. 'There you go,' said Barnaby, tapping Samantha's cage with his cane. 'Now, you two can have some nice conversations. You will both be lovely attractions; Samantha, an example of the greed and infantile thinking that stems from a belief in Santa. Randall, you will stand as an example of a once-mighty animal brought down to earth. Just think of all the children that will finally see the light!'

'So,' said Randall, 'You want kids to stop believing in Santa or…'

'I'm showing them the error of their ways! I'm showing them the truth behind their squabbling and gluttony! What I'm doing is no different from what Diane does! And of course, my little lesson will be during the day, when people are more likely to pay attention to it too! A shame she got away, maybe we could have figured something out.'

Some time later, Samantha came to and shrieked her head off at finding herself in a cage, with Carl, Derek and Barnaby all chortling at it. 'Listen to her,' said Derek, pulling out a cigarette. 'She sounds like one of them monkeys at the zoo.'

Randall fell to the floor of his cage, rolling his eyes. 'Samantha,' he said, 'You wouldn't happen to remember the spell to remove this cage, do you?'

Samantha took a break from her shrieking and began to chuckle. 'Even if I did,' she said, 'you'd think I'd use it to help you?'

'Come, come!' Barnaby clapped his hands. 'You two, be quiet! Santa, get your face out of your hands this instant! This is going to be quite an eventful night for you, my friend. I mean, we do have more of your helpers to resurrect!'

Out on the streets again, out and about in this robe. Diane thought about something else to wear – veil, hoodie, even the classic trenchcoat and hat – but all she could do with her clothing at the moment was make her robe disappear, and make it reappear. She could probably take her dress off too, but even here she had respect for public decency laws. Though she did briefly consider running down the streets starkers, screaming and telling people to change their ways or she'd eat their flesh, she kept that fantasy to herself.

Usually she had a photographic memory, a list of the mortals she had visited like Santa's list of all the people he delivered to. You had to know your enemy, you had to think like your enemy, but now, Diane found her mind all scrambled. She tried thinking of one thing, but that transformed into another. She tried thinking of anything that could lead her to help, and suddenly she remembered a song she liked out of nowhere.

Bloody brain. Come on.

She was certain this street was where the Christmas festival was being held. She was certain this is where Randall died. Throughout her afterlife, Diane had seen several people die, and she remembered all of them. A lot of them she had tried to save, with Randall being the latest in a long line. The stage where Randall played her was over there. The road where his life was taken was over there. The church where his funeral was held was not too far from here.

Diane ran across the road, darting into shadow after shadow, until she finally reached the church. When she saw it, she wondered how strange it would look if she didn't have her robe on and there was a living corpse walking through a holy place. She thought she didn't look too out of place with her robe, since some said it made her look like a monk, but now was not the time to focus on that.

Diane had been to Randall's funeral, and when it was over, she left with everyone to a gathering afterwards, and she was certain his ex – Alice – went back to a flat not too far from here. Diane was even certain she followed her, because she seemed to be crying the most.

There it was. There was the flat. Diane dove for it, slipping through the walls of the flat. She may have had her power of the future nullified and she may have been trapped on this plane for the time being, but she still could search buildings quickly, and was as shifty as ever. Through the corridor she glided, taking quick peeks here and there until she could sense that she was close to Alice, feeling a little familiar twinge.

She had been here before. Several times. The residents of this flat had been screwed over by their bosses and other people in power, and Diane had showed the residents of this flat *to* those bosses and other people in power. She was pretty sure she even remembered most of their names…Alice was one of them too, wasn't she? Her boss needed to give her more time off because the stress was getting to her. When he died of a heart attack, she didn't mourn his death, and *here's her flat right here.*

It didn't look all that different from when Diane showed an apathetic Alice. In fact, the lights were still on, and Alice was lying on the sofa, watching a taped version of *10 O'Clock Live*.

What else could she do?

'Aaaalice! Aaaalice!'

She fell off her sofa, and when she sprung up, she did look a little more awake. 'Lenny?' she said, 'Is that you?'

'Alice!' Instantly, Diane shed her cloak and now there was a living skeleton in a dress walking towards Alice. Why not? If she revealed herself at a pub, why not there and then? People were probably twittering about it right now. They were probably also twittering about seeing their dead relatives…

Alice screamed. At least it looked like she was screaming, no sound came out of her mouth except a slight wheeze. She stood, frozen in place.

'Oh, you're one of *those* people. Anyway, you need to come with me. It's Randall.'

Alice began to twitch.

'I know where Randall is, and he's in danger. I need someone to help save him.'

'Are…are…'

'Are? R? S?'

'Are you…Death?'

'Um, sure, let's go with that. Anyway, when Randall died, he went into the afterlife as a…oh just come with me. I'm not sure how much time we have left.'

With a click of her fingers, Diane once again shrouded herself in her robe and ran out through the flat, waiting for Alice to catch up. Seeing no sign of her, she ran back into the flat and poked her head through the door to see Alice still standing. 'Come along or I'll eat your flesh.'

Alice went along.

Sleep. Randall needed sleep. Such a thing surprised him, as he was certain that in the movies, ghosts didn't need sleep. He was pretty sure he thought reindeer didn't need to sleep too, considering how much energy they seemed to have in the stories. Yet now that he was a ghost reindeer, he had never felt more fatigue in his l…in ever.

Yet it seemed like Barnaby had plenty of energy to spare; taking the graveyard shift – no pun intended – while Carl and Derek had their kip. He sat by Samantha, Santa and Randall on a dusty old armchair, leaning on his cane, a book in his lap. Just before sending off Carl and Derek to bed, he had whispered a few more spells for good measure.

If Barnaby wasn't going to sleep, Randall wasn't going to sleep, no matter how much he felt his non-existent bones ache. Santa was fast asleep though, but he deserved a rest after all he had been through. Samantha looked like she was asleep, but Randall knew she was awake, most likely trying to remember any spells she could. Most likely any that would either kill Barnaby or do something just as bad to Randall.

There were other reindeer as well, in several candy floss cages, those who followed Randall's example and refused resurrection. Billy was there, flopping about his cage, vainly attempting to sleep. He was told to come here by Samantha, and as soon as he saw Santa, he flew up and yelled at Barnaby in his face. Seeing the plump reindeer in this state made Randall almost want to leap out, but not only was he restrained by the bars, but by Barnaby's glare as well.

Barnaby continued to stare, rocking his cane a little. He didn't say, 'I know you're awake' but that's all Randall could hear when he looked at him. With the way his teeth jutted out from his lips, he didn't even need to open his mouth to render Randall silent.

Randall had to look at Barnaby, though. Barnaby had magic, two helpers and a ruthless attitude at his disposal; the guy needed about twenty CCTV cameras hovering above him at all times. It was either Randall or Samantha who was going to watch him, and Randall wouldn't trust Samantha to watch over his shoes.

As long as Randall stared at Barnaby, he didn't move, except a little wriggle of his cane. This only gave Randall more incentive to stare at Barnaby; he was reminded of that one TV show he watched a while ago about the evil statues that only moved when you looked at them.

'Samantha,' he croaked, finally moving at last. 'Are we comfy in there?' She was still awake, Randall knew, but she chose to lie down and not answer. 'Youth today,' sneered Barnaby. 'Though at least you're quiet. That's something at least.' He went back to his seat and continued to stare at Randall.

At least until he heard glass breaking.

'Oho!' he cried, right before standing upwards. 'We appear to have company. Is that you, Diane, here to be the big heroine?' He heard much banging and bumping in the other room. 'Even if it isn't Diane,' he said, 'I know it's my prisoners you're after, so why don't you simply come in here and get them?'

Randall heard mumbling from the other room; one voice was clearly Diane's, but another...

'Hey!' Randall yelled.

'You be quiet!' snapped Barnaby, 'There's no need to yell, they're coming for you anyway!'

Ignoring Barnaby, Randall cried out for attention again anyway, and a voice cried back, 'Randall?'

'Alice! In here!'

The door to the room burst open, and there stood Alice, parka and all, staring in disbelief. 'Randall?'

'Oh,' said Barnaby, eying Alice as she slowly backed away. 'Looks like the cavalry has come, haven't they? You know Randall here? He may not be as you used to recognise him, however.'

Alice looked as if she was about to run away, only for Barnaby to grab her by the wrist and force her down onto the ground. First her face was brought up against Santa's cage so she could see the symbol of the holiday in an uneasy slumber. Then, as his fingers tightened around her skull, she was brought face to face with Randall the reindeer.

'Alice,' said Randall, bringing his face closer to the light, but not close that he'd touch the bars of his cage. 'It's me, Randall.'

'Randall?' She reached in to touch him, but pulled away her hand upon receiving a shock from the cage. 'What have they done to you?'

'Don't you mean,' said Barnaby, pointing to the ceiling before pointing at Santa, 'what has *he* done to Randall? He is a tyrant, my dear, forcing everyone to think like he does. I'm really trying to save him, but considering he refused my offer to bring him back to life, I think it may be too late.'

'Wait?' said Alice, pulling herself away. 'You're bringing the dead back to life? What...what is all this?'

'Something that I fear may be difficult to understand for you,' he said, 'but I can resurrect your little friend here. If only he'd agree.'

Randall looked up at Alice. 'I can't...I can't...'

'I dunno,' said Alice, 'I just thought if you were given a choice to be brought back, you'd take it. I mean, your mum really misses you...'

'I doubt Mum wants to see a zombie though,' replied Randall.

'Speaking of undead,' said Barnaby, 'I know *she's* here. Come out, come out, wherever you are.' He stood up straight – he was straight one second, crooked the next – and took a look around the room. The way he searched made him look more like a vulture than he usually did. 'Come on out, we don't have to be enemies, you know. We have a lot in common, really.'

'Rubbish,' came a voice.

'I understand you better than most people do,' said Barnaby, 'Your goal is not to make people "nice" per se, rather to make them wiser.' Barnaby walked away to a corner of the room, taking his cane, but leaving his book behind. When he did, Randall poked a hoof-hand through one of the cage's few openings and gestured towards it to Alice. Alice picked it up.

'You show visions of terror,' Barnaby continued, 'visions of death, because you want people to stop being greedy. This is what I'm doing. Once they see the symbol of their avarice treated like a sideshow attraction, they'll realise how worthless it truly all is. What does Santa do except give things that will merely be grown out of? If he was truly the figure of love he purports to be, why did he not let me write something other than *Edward the Duck*? Why not give out one of my political essays?'

Alice, making sure not to sit on the chair as it looked pretty creaky, flicked through the spell book in order to find something that would free Randall. She looked at a spell to make shoes as good as new, a spell to reverse aging, and, when she flicked to the back, a double page spell for resurrecting the dead. Something that clearly stated would restore the body of a spirit.

'Are you sure…' whispered Alice, holding the book up so Randall could see the spell.

Randall was just about to say 'no' but then his mind forced him to think back. His death was a mistake, and mistakes had to be rectified. If he had just been a little more careful when going about his dance, he'd be at home right now, enjoying his holidays, having a good night's kip after watching *How the Grinch Stole Christmas* for the billionth time.

'Oi!' came a voice. 'You're supposed to say no. Find the spell to free him, Alice!'

'Ah! There you are!' Barnaby pointed his cane towards a shadow, between Randall's cage and Samantha's. Diane slunk out, wearing her robe again. 'Now come out and play.' In a second, he snatched away the spell book from Alice and held it under his arm.

At that, Alice decided that she would repay the favour. As

quick as she could, she snatched away Barnaby's cane and sent him tumbling to the floor. ⤢

'Huh,' said Diane, shrugging, 'Why didn't I think of that?' Just then, her eye caught the human Samantha in the orthodox cage. 'Hey! I know you!'

Samantha finally revealed that she was awake. 'Oh, it's you. What do you want?'

'You really did it, didn't you? I doubt you'd be going back to Purgatory now. You definitely won't be ascending.'

'So what if I'm going to Hell? I'd rather go to Hell than that sugary wasteland Santa calls a home.'

'This is exactly what I showed your father, you know. You growing selfish and abrasive because of how much he spoiled you. You didn't even care about his death.'

'Well, he's dead now, and I did bloody well care, so there you are, mission accomplished. Look!' She gestured towards her dress. 'I did this sort of stuff to help me forget that he was attacked while on one of those little errands you inspired him to do, leaving us even worse off than we were when he gave away half our money!'

Diane took off her hood and scowled at her. 'You know something very important I've learned in my career? That some people cannot be redeemed. I make sure I haunt people who can take a lesson, but that number has decreased in the last few years, hasn't it? It's gotten to the point where one person's redemption leads to someone else becoming even worse.'

Samantha deflated. 'Okay, just get me out of here. I'll go away and put this necromancy stuff behind me, I swear.'

'No,' Diane glared. 'You got yourself into this mess. What your father chose to do was because of him, not me. You practicing necromancy is because of you. Not me. You can die of malnutrition in that cage for all I care.'

'Come on!' cried Samantha, 'If you get me out, I'll go away and never come back! I'll forget all the spells and mumbo jumbo, and go back to my mum!'   '

'You really think you're going to adequately explain this to your mother without her freaking out?' said Diane. 'Either she'll think you're a zombie or she'll know you've been participating in the black arts. People freaked out when they saw me, and they didn't even know who I was when I was alive!' A snide smile then crept across her face. 'Maybe it'd be better for you if you died again. Richest girl in the cemetery.'

'No, come on! My mum will be happy to see me! I know she's been praying to see me again! And it's as a human, not a ruddy reindeer! I've learned my lesson, I really have!'

'I'm not stupid!' roared Diane. 'I know when people have learned their lesson and I know the moment you get out, you'll grab that book and trap me in another cage. Well, you can just forget it. In fact,' she added, looking away from Samantha, 'you lot can solve your own problems.' With that, she walked out through the wall.

While Diane and Samantha were having that little conversation, Alice had pried the book from Barnaby's hands, and as Barnaby was making his way up, Alice flicked through page after page. 'Look for any cage pictures,' said Randall.

'I know that,' replied Alice just as she came across one. 'Okay, I think I found it, oh yeah, here's how to reverse it I think…'

Barnaby, now back on his feet, pounded his palm on the book and growled. 'It takes a certain type of person to perform this magic well, my dear, and I fear you are much too mundane.' Alice closed the book and raised it above her head. 'Don't you try anything,' said Barnaby, 'I still have other spells, you know.' Hopping over to the bookcase, he pulled out a piece of parchment. 'During my time alive,' said Barnaby, flapping the piece of paper about, 'I've forgotten more about this art then you'll ever know, and my new friends aren't that bad at it either. One false move, and your friend gets cast into an endless oblivion!'

Alice slowly brought the book down to her waist, and took another look at Randall. His eyes were wide and he looked about the room like a frightened dog. When Alice opened the book again, Barnaby croaked out the first two verses of a spell. A black blot formed on the bottom of Randall's cage. It reminded Alice of the Black Spot from *Treasure Island*. It looked more like a mark on the cage's floor than an actual physical puddle, but Alice swore she could see a little claw sprout from it. She looked into the book and heard squelching sounds and a whimper from Randall's throat.

'All right,' said Alice, her hands and lips trembling as she handed the book back to Barnaby.

'Thank you,' said Barnaby, smiling so his eyes grew wider and his wrinkles grew deeper. Just as soon as he received the book, he heard blubbering, which made his eyes and wrinkles grow even more. Samantha was sitting up, holding her legs, trying to hold back tears.

'Oh, really now. You're a big girl, start acting like it.' He cackled, but then he heard slight mumbling from behind him. Familiar mumbling at that. 'She didn't.'

Randall's cage disappeared. Well, not all of it, just one or two or three bars, seeing how the spell was spoken, and Randall bounced out just in time to come face to face with an angry Barnaby, who was beginning to mouth something.

'Run run run!' Randall darted away, and Alice followed after him, leaping through the window she had broken, tumbling down onto her knees when she landed on the pavement. The growl of Barnaby, however, had her immediately back on her feet, running alongside Randall until both of them dove into an alleyway. 'Geez,' said Randall, rubbing his face. 'I can't breathe anymore and yet I feel out of breath. Thanks for freeing me, Alice.'

'What do we do now?' said Alice, after she had managed to regain most of her breath.

'You wouldn't happen to still remember that spell that freed me, would you?'

'Bugger,' said Alice, hitting her head like it was a TV on the fritz. 'It's completely gone.' She tried to recite it again, only for it to turn into gibberish.

'Well,' said Randall. 'If I'm free of that cage, I should be able to get back to Purgatory and maybe get some help. Just a sec.' Randall scrunched up his face in a way that made him look constipated, rubbing his head and repeating 'Purgatory' over and over, but as hard as he tried, he remained in the alleyway.

'So you can't even do that?'

'Wait,' said Randall, raising a hoof. 'Let me try something.' He clacked his feet together like Dorothy clacked together the ruby slippers, and slowly levitated a few inches above the ground. 'Hey, I still have it!' He struck a superhero pose and then took off to the skies like a rocket, flying in circles above the alleyway before setting himself back down.

Alice folded her arms. 'That's all well and good, but aren't we supposed to be saving Santa and those others?' She then just realised she had finally gotten used to all these goings-on and thought for a minute that perhaps she should be proud of herself. 'Has Death really bailed on us?'

'Seems that way.'

Hearing this, Alice laid her head against a wall, and took a deep sigh. 'Maybe we should just go to the police about this. I've got a talking reindeer right here, they'd believe me.'

'That'd be open season to him,' came a familiar voice, 'all those policemen just ready to be annihilated with his magic. He never sleeps, believe me, I've watched him.' From behind a bin, there slunk Diane, robe and all. Alice jumped slightly. 'He's like one of those guards at Buckingham Palace, only much more effective. If the police had half his focus, crime'd be down at least seventy-five percent.'

'I thought you had abandoned us,' said Randall.

'That's what I want Samantha to think,' said Diane, with a little playful laugh. 'She could stand to learn something. Maybe then they'll go a little easier on her.'

Randall arched his head. 'Well, I think we should help her.'

'We will,' replied Diane, 'we just have to wait for the right time.'

'Well,' said Randall, 'when will that be?'

'First,' said Diane, 'We have to wait until we can be sure Samantha will help us. Also, now is not really a good time to try an attack or anything like that. Barnaby and those two friends of his outclass us, especially since Barnaby still has a bit of Hell's power in him. Plus, at this time, Barnaby is giving his scheme full attention. When he carries out his plan in the morning, he'll likely be flushed with victory and then he'd be easier to surprise. I've pretty much exposed myself already, heck, I think we're exposing ourselves right now.'

'Okay,' said Alice. 'Is there anything you want me to do?'

'Of course,' said Diane, making Alice's stomach sink, 'We need a human to read out any spells they have, so we can reverse them. I still need to get back my power of showing possible futures by next night.' Alice turned to Diane with a quizzical expression. 'Oh, yes, I'm not really Death, you know. I'm the Ghost of Christmas Yet to Come. Yes, from the Dickens book, and yes, that was Barnaby from *Babes in Toyland*. Would you ask that, though?'

'Oh god,' sighed Alice, facing the wall again. 'This is something out of *Abbott and Costello*, isn't it?'

'I can tell you're exhausted by what's going on,' said Diane, 'Maybe you should go back to your flat for a rest, so you'll be energised for tomorrow. Perhaps you should let Randall stay with you too.' Randall nodded. 'A shame you can't touch Randall...that came out wrong...I meant, if he wasn't a spirit, you could ride on his back.'

'You really think he should be flying about?'

'Well,' Randall butted in. 'Barnaby and Samantha...well, are doing all this to humiliate Santa. I just thought if any kids saw me flying about and I told them something like, "Hey, just practicing for tomorrow", they'd think Santa was still at the North Pole and then they'd be more likely to think the Santa Barnaby'll be parading about isn't the real Santa. I mean, even when I was a kid, I knew the shopping centre Santas weren't real. If kids don't think he's the real Santa, Barnaby's plan will fail.'

'He'll still have Santa in a cage, and a good amount of necromancy on his side,' said Diane, 'though I suppose every little helps in these types of situations. Okay, we all go to Alice's flat and get some rest, then wait until Barnaby makes his move.'

Thus, they all did as Diane suggested, with Diane slinking in the shadows, Alice simply walking, and Randall flying about. He looked as if he was on a silo, lounging about. Alice saw him flying on his back, looking relaxed. When Alice passed by one or two people, they didn't seem to notice either Randall or Diane. Maybe they thought Randall was a decoration that got blown away or something.

Alice soon reached her flat and found Diane and Randall there waiting for her, both of them sitting on the sofa. Seeing them there, Alice could do nothing else but ask, 'Why is it that you're not going through the sofa when you go through everything else?'

'Yeah,' said Randall, 'I was...' At that, he fell right through the sofa.

'It's one of those things that works more the less you think about it,' said Diane, standing up so the same didn't happen to her. 'Some things on Earth work better than others for us spirits. Sadly, guns aren't one of them. We can't eat Earth foods because we can go on without eating, but we can stand on Earth ground because spirit bodies are so used to standing on Purgatory ground, and are used to sitting, that the body instinctively mimics sitting down. We can all float, but not to the extent to how Randall now can.'

To emphasise this, Randall flew about the ceiling again.

'Forget everything I said,' said Diane.

Randall came down to the floor. 'Done.'

'If you two have bickered enough,' said Alice, 'I'm going to sleep.'

'Good idea,' said Randall, and lay down in the air, closing his eyes so he didn't see Diane and Alice roll theirs.

Santa had lived for years and years and decades in a place filled with snow and ice, and yet, even though sunlight shone on him, he felt cold. Though he was currently wearing his classic red coat, he held himself and shook, watching as Carl and Derek spoke with Barnaby about the preparations they were making.

Not wishing to listen to their voices any longer, Santa instead turned his attention to his other reindeer. Though he admired the fact that they were unwilling to participate in this bizarre ritual, he had a good mind to try and break through the bars of his cage just to see if he could break through theirs. He closed his eyes, and put his hand through the thorny bars. Electricity crackled through his body, and it felt like nails were being hammered into his arms through his palms, but he continued. He hummed 'Here Comes Santa Claus' to himself to lessen the pain, and despite the agony surging, he felt like he had managed to get his palm through.

All of a sudden, a powerful blast of energy sent him flying backwards.

'Oh, I was so waiting for him to do that,' said Barnaby to his friends. 'I must say, you have done a magnificent job with the cages' magic. It seemed I underestimated you. Now, have you got our attention-grabbers ready?'

Every word that came out of Barnaby's mouth stung Santa's ears as much as the bars stung his arms, so he focussed on the reindeer again, especially his once most-trusted one. Samantha lay huddled in her cage, and Santa could tell she was genuinely fast asleep. Even from here, Santa could tell her eyes were red from crying, and she had been scratching her face in frustration. Though it was Samantha that had landed Santa in this cage, he wanted to open Samantha's cage and comfort her, hold her in his arms. Then perhaps she would be sorry for what she had done. Kindness always helped change people better than fear ever did; when would Diane learn that?

Burying his head away from the sight of Barnaby and the caged reindeer, Santa began to remember his early years. Back when he had discovered the true joy of Christmas, giving – and even making – toys for children who could use them felt like a weight lifted from his stomach, shackles cast away from him. In fact, his death wasn't what one could call a death, but more a rebirth, a different life as a different person. He was slim and clean-shaven in his first life, and in Purgatory, he had a belly like a bowl full of jelly and a big fluffy beard, the perfect image of the kindly grandpa.

Many of Purgatory's people were children or they needed to be reminded of their childhood in order to get better adjusted to this plane. Thus, Santa was given an entire realm to assure the delivery of presents on one of the nights spirits were at their most powerful. Those who had died shortly after him were made into elves, those who would assist in the creation of toys and other presents, and reindeer, who would help take Santa around the near-endless world of Purgatory. There were plenty of people in Purgatory and a lot of them wanted presents and upon Santa's request, welcomed him into their homes. Some, though, preferred that Santa paid a housecall in the morning and delivered the presents personally, to avoid something that resembled home invasion.

His first outing went off without a hitch. The elves had made all the toys, all the musical instruments, all the various knick-knacks ahead of time, and though he was deceased and delivered at night, Santa had never felt so much energy. All the regrets of the past, all the memories of his misdeeds had been snuffed out just like the light of a candle.

The next year felt just the same, with Santa even considering beginning the rounds an hour before he was supposed to. Before that, he had made sure all his helpers felt the same joy as he did. Not only did the elves build toys, they helped Santa in building a lot more houses in the realm and improving the ones already there. Many reindeer in this realm were shocked to find themselves in the form of hooved animals when they came here, so the least Santa could do was make them feel more comfortable in their new forms.

The second year was another success, and on Christmas Day, Santa gave all his elves and reindeer a well-deserved rest, and even gave them all presents he had made himself. His Christmas Day he planned to spend in the office, reading the books he had been given from the authors of Toyland, but that plan was interrupted by the entrance of a skeleton in a dress, looking at him with eyeballs popping from her sockets. She sat on his desk, staring at him. Though she seemed to have eyelids, she didn't blink.

'Well,' she said, 'It seems your career here is coming along well. It's a shame you didn't ascend right away; maybe it was all those things you did in the past that were holding you back.'

Santa forced himself to look at this woman, and asked, 'Who are you?'

'Don't you remember?' she said, and made a robe appear on her body. One which hid her face and her form, revealing only her skeletal hands. It could be none other.

'You're the Ghost of Christmas Yet to Come,' gasped Santa.

'Yes,' said the Ghost, giving herself back her normal dress, 'but you can call me Diane. You know, you are probably my greatest success. I mean, I was actually offered ascension because of you.'

'Then why are you still here?'

Diane's expression became anxious. 'It just didn't feel right.'

'Well,' said Santa, 'I think you deserve to ascend, you did help me see the light after all.'

'Thank you,' replied Diane. Santa swore he saw a bit of a blush on her skull. 'I really think you'll ascend one day as well.' She turned to the desk and saw the book. 'I'm not disturbing anything, am I?'

'No, no.'

She looked at the book's title. 'A little too old to be reading this sort of thing, aren't you?'

'If I'm going to deliver to children,' said Santa, 'I should know what they like.'

'Fair enough,' replied Diane. 'I was mostly here just to see how you were doing, anyway. I'll leave if I'm being too much of a bother.'

'No, no,' said Santa, waving his hand about. 'Stay a while, I could use someone to talk to.'

'I know what you mean,' replied Diane. 'Some people have been avoiding me due to my job, and I think I could use some social interaction here and there. Say, I know a really good place to eat in the other end of Purgatory. Maybe when you're not too busy, we can go there and have a conversation.'

Santa agreed, and on Boxing Day, they found themselves eating at the restaurant. It was a casual affair, so neither of them dressed too fancy. No-one commented on their casual wear, just how strange it seemed to see a jolly old man and a skeleton together, even in Purgatory. They sat together by the window, where they had a good view of the bright white clouds against the inky blackness of the sky. Diane said it was beautiful in its own way, but the sight of it stung Santa's eyes.

'You know,' said Diane, drumming her fingers on her chin, 'I really do like the symbolism you utilize. I wonder if it was inspired by Norse mythology.'

'How do you mean?'

'I remember hearing that the gods Thor and Odin were supposed to have white beards, and Thor had a chariot pulled by goats like you have a sleigh pulled by reindeer,' said Diane. 'Since I've heard of Purgatory being mistaken for Valhalla, I wonder if they were inspired by that.'

'There have been legends of someone like me on Earth already,' replied Santa, 'that's what they seem to be borrowing from.'

'I see,' said Diane.

'Did you not borrow your image from the legends of Death as well?'

'I suppose I did,' replied Diane. 'I was just saying that you have some striking imagery with you. You are a mighty God, soaring through the skies, power in your wrists.'

'That does sound quite intimidating,' said Santa, shirking back slightly. 'My goal is to bring joy to others.'

'You can bring fear and joy,' said Diane. 'That's what horror stories were intended to do.'

'I have never liked horror stories,' said Santa, 'there is too much horror in the world already without it invading our fiction.'

'The horror of the world has awoken people to the needs of others, though.'

'Who then try to end that horror.'

'Fear stops people from doing bad things. If they end real horror, it is because they are afraid of more real horror happening. The people of Purgatory fear descent, so they do everything they can to avoid it.'

'People do not ascend merely because they are afraid of descent, but because they genuinely want to do good.'

'Indeed,' said Diane, 'but sometimes fear can be the only way they'll really pay any attention to you. Does not God use it? Fear God?'

Before the conversation could continue, their food arrived, and they silently ate it. They left without saying a word to each other.

They tried again to have a night out the following year, when neither of them had ascended, and since the conversation was on a different topic than fear, there were more smiles and a better atmosphere than the last meal, so they tried again the next year, when Santa noticed Diane hanging her head.

When asked what was wrong, she replied, 'I was just thinking of my mother. I did all I could to help support her. I even…' Then she got a good look at Santa, and ran away.

It wasn't until later that Santa learned that he had met Diane when they both were alive. He had seen her on the streets shortly before she died, and he had rejected to aid her. It was about a few days after the death of her mother – who had instantly descended after her death – too. Diane had told Santa it didn't really bother her, that she was more concerned with how Santa was now then he was back then, but seeing Diane had always given him a sting.

That sting seemed to linger for years, and he wondered if that was one the reasons he hadn't ascended. Over time he continued to deliver presents, and yet, it didn't seem to carry the joy it used to. It was about after his twentieth year that the magic began to trickle out of the proceedings. This alone filled Santa with dread; if he wasn't filled with joy, how could he bring joy to others? If he was filled with fear, wouldn't he bring fear to others?

A harsh shudder brought Santa back to the present to see Carl and Derek lifting him onto what looked like a poorly-constructed parade float, with streamers, large arrows, and right next to Santa was a box that looked vaguely familiar.

A box from Purgatory.

Would it be of any use to them?

'Are you comfortable, Santa?' Barnaby hopped onto the float and took a good gander. 'My, my, aren't we pathetic, but still, if someone said you were the real article, I would believe them. After all, have not the dead risen recently?' Barnaby held up a radio. 'Just heard the news. Christopher Walton was a soldier who died on the battlefield on Christmas Eve. Three years later to the day, he returns to his parents to their joy and shock. A mother knows her son, and she is insisting he is the real deal. A woman saw her husband knifed by a murderer, and someone who could only be her husband came to her door at 1am.

'News travels fast, doesn't it? It's morning on Christmas Eve and already these resurrections have become widely public. People on Twitter have been accusing these people of faking their deaths or being imposters, but several are calling it a "Christmas miracle", or a "sign of the apocalypse". People have gathered to the church as soon as it opened. This Christmas Eve, for them, is one where anything can happen, so they're likely to believe that the real Santa Claus has been captured, especially since he has talking reindeer with him, and we'll have a little show as well.' He patted the box next to Santa.

'What's that?'

'Oh, this? Something we tested the resurrection spell upon. Turns out it's a bit more lenient on inanimate objects.' He patted it.

'You know they have special effect technicians in Purgatory? Well, our good friend Samantha procured some of "Paul's" best wares, so people will pay attention to us. If the people didn't think the world was ending now, wait until they see these! Diane is right, you see, sometimes people will only listen to them if you scare them first!'

Samantha was loaded onto the truck – Santa gave a quick look around and saw that it wasn't a float as he initially thought, just a truck with decorations – and so were those who refused resurrection. Almost the second everyone was on the truck, Carl and Derek began to drive it onto the streets, while Barnaby presided over the cages.

It took no time at all for them to reach a busy street. Barnaby opened the box.

The spectres that arose resembled three-dimensional versions of Halloween cartoon ghosts, only more so. They were living bedsheets draped over giant skulls, stained with filth and with long mouths that stretched as long as a foot. They shrieked and hollered, but they begged the screaming men and women to pay attention to the truck. Arms sprung from their tattered form, as 'See' emanated from their elongated mouths.

'People!' Barnaby yelled on a megaphone. 'You have ruined Christmas! What was supposed to be a holiday of generosity and joy has become one of greed and selfishness! And who is enabling this attitude? Santa Claus! The man who has turned your children into materialistic monsters, jabbering and squabbling for the latest disposable playthings! He who has drained your wallet and your soul! Well, now here he lies! Him and his helpers!'

From his pocket, Barnaby got out a Taser and turned it on. In seconds, he used it on Billy, revealing his fierce but human scream to everyone. 'This is not a reindeer, at least, he wasn't born one. Santa has been harvesting the souls of the dead and has been forcing them to work under his cruel regime! I have been giving back life to some of them, but many are so far gone they have refused my help, and must be punished!'

Barnaby looked down to see people approaching the truck, only to get knocked back by the magic Carl and Derek had cast on the vehicle. 'Do not try and save these scoundrels,' cried Barnaby into the megaphone. 'Instead, let Santa, caged and pathetic as he is now, serve as an example as what happens to those who misuse the Christmas spirit! Let him now be a symbol of how so many of you have corrupted the holiday! It is better to give than to receive, and I am giving you an important lesson in the Christmas spirit.'

Now that he knew just how powerful his cage was, Santa tried his best not to touch the bars. Still, his hands trembled with the desire to break through them. To release his reindeer and bring them back to Purgatory. To throttle Barnaby.

It was Diane that woke up Randall and Alice, jolting them from their slumber with a loud shriek, a horrific wail one would expect from the monsters Diane resembled. Randall had spent the whole night in the air, while Alice had been told to sleep in her clothes – 'We have worse things to worry about then body odor,' said Diane – but neither of them felt tired when they saw Diane sitting next to the TV.

'Can you believe the media?' she said, kicking her legs in the air. Alice took a look at her position and saw that, yes, she was hovering slightly above the chair. 'We're barely into Christmas Eve and already they're saying it's the end times. Seriously, people know about the dead coming back, and they know about Paul's little effects that Samantha bought. I was pretty sure I was even mentioned once or twice. "I saw Death walking down the streets towards the pub." I suppose I should be flattered.'

'That's all well and good,' said Alice, still feeling a slight throbbing from sleeping all night in her clothes, 'but what are we going to do about Barnaby and Santa?'

'Well,' said Diane. 'First of all, you have to go back to the medium's and see if you can find any spell books that can release Santa and the reindeer, and reverse the spells they put on me and Randall so we can go back to Purgatory. Those three are so confident in this plan, they'll likely have neglected to take all their books. Randall, I think you may have had a point; try to see if you can convince these people that that is not the real Santa, just so we don't get any traumatized kids.'

Randall saluted, and then asked, 'What are you going to do?'

'I'll think of something,' Diane snapped, waving her hands about. 'Just go, go, go! We don't have enough time!'

Randall flew out of the window. Lucky him, thought Alice, as she ran downstairs from her flat. Just as she thought it, she looked up and saw ugly spectres soaring at ground level. She wondered if she should thank Diane; having a skeleton stay a night in your flat makes creatures like these seem all the less striking.

Alice would have liked to have run to Barnaby's lair, but that would be difficult considering how many other people were running.

The spirits approached them and they ran away…no, they ran towards the ghosts. The ghosts were beckoning them to come, and they were. Though she doubted how much it would help, she pulled the hood of her parka up, and squinted slightly. When she came onto the streets, she didn't run, but rather jogged. In fact, Alice felt like she was in a video game, where she had to avoid all the obstacles and stop the villains. That made her situation seem no less ridiculous, but it at least kept her spirits up.

Suddenly, she began to dance.

Her legs danced, at least. Though she was in control of her upper body, her legs had gained a mind of their own, moving in odd directions to one of the phantoms. The ghost floated above the ground, beckoning to her with its skeletal finger – its bones more yellow and rotted than Diane's – and saying, 'Come with me.'

The more it whispered, the more Alice found herself approaching it in her discordant fashion. Her legs gyrated and warped and walked towards the beast and its hanging mouth until she made a wonky step and fell to the ground, her arm passing through the ghost. Her arm passing through the ghost felt different than it did when it passed through Randall and Diane; she didn't feel a presence. There was no weight to this creature; it was about as real as the spooks on a funfair ghost train.

With that in mind, Alice found herself regaining control of her legs, and instinctively running in a more coherent fashion. Given that she was led to Barnaby's hideout only about a few hours ago, she was pretty sure she knew the way there, but then again, on her first journey there, all she really thought about was the fact that she was following Death to find the ghost of her ex-boyfriend.

She was pretty sure she passed this building on the first trip, but in which direction? It was this way, no, this? The attempts to piece together a path and the yelling, running, dancing people around her made Alice feel dizzy, so she leaned against a wall.

Still she saw the phantoms. Still she heard them call for followers and beckon with their rotted fingers. Though she no longer felt any urge to follow them, seeing and hearing them tugged at her insides and made her lose focus on finding her goal.

It didn't take long for her to get her head on straight though, and she simply told herself to ignore the ghosts and pretend that the people around her were just going to a concert or something. She usually completed a goal better when she temporarily forgot why she wanted to accomplish that goal, so for the time being she forgot that she found out about ghosts and told herself that she was going to the medium's simply because she wanted to.

Ah yes, there was another landmark she pretty sure was near her destination. The Co-Op. Not just any Co-Op, the small one. Near where she lived there was a big one and a small one, and Alice was sure the destination was closer to the small one than the big one. She was even certain she had been in that area several times while out on a stroll.

After ducking from the spectres and diving through crowds of people, Alice found the shop, still with its window broken. After double-checking to make sure people were paying more attention to the strange goings-on than to her, she leapt right in and walked towards where she had seen Randall being kept. She had never really given the place a good look when she had seen Randall here, and thus she noticed how dusty it was. Not because it was a mystical place of magic, but rather because the owners weren't much for cleaning up after themselves. Magical artifacts lay among old pop culture memorabilia, and the bookshelf wasn't in that good shape either. Still, that was what Alice was after.

She pulled out the thickest, filthiest book in the shelf, a page falling out as she did so. However, when she picked up the page, it turned out to be a cookbook. The next book she pulled out was a hardcover *Star Wars* encyclopedia, and the one after that was completely blank except for a grocery list.

Thus she tried the next shelf. Ah. The first book she pulled from the next shelf was a spell book, and as she flicked through it, she saw pictures of cages and of ghosts. When she turned to the page with the picture of the cage, she looked over the spell, and yes, it was what she had used to free Randall. She would have left there and then, but her body was frozen in place and without a ghost to be found too.

All of a sudden, Alice began to remember what had led her here. Not only had she met the ghost of her dead ex-boyfriend, but said ghost was a talking reindeer. All the characters from the corny cartoons Randall liked to watch even in adulthood had been brought to life. Also, Alice held the power of the universe in her hands. Something endlessly potent some idiots had left for her to have for herself.

With this book, she could make things appear and disappear from thin air, summon nightmarish visions, and even bring the dead back to life. Were the ghost of William Shakespeare to come to her, all she had to do was read out a few words and the world would have the Bard back. She even had the power to undo Randall's death, and he was reluctant to let her. Strange that.

'What are you doing here?' came a familiar whisper that shook Alice's head back onto the physical plane. Not only was she here, but so was a pseudo-ghost, beckoning her to come. Looking down at her feet, Alice saw she was still, and thus considered flicking through the book to see if there were any spells that would dispel the vision. Then she remembered this thing was supposed to lead her to Barnaby, and all she said was 'Lead the way.'   •

Bloody phantoms, bloody phantoms, thought Randall as he ascended higher and higher. He flew so high he could barely see the streets below – which defeated the purpose of him coming up here in the first place – but it did give him a brief reprieve from the pointing, the beckoning, and how his legs seemed to twist and turn whenever they were around.

He thought of simply jettisoning the mission and staying in the clouds, just to see how Earth's sky differed from the one in Purgatory, but instead, he hovered in the air and waited for the ghosts to clear. Every time the mere thought of abandoning the mission popped into his mind, that was followed by a thought about what Diane would think. Her expressive skull was burned into his brain.

He hovered, and couldn't help but notice how light he felt. It reminded him of when he and Alice went to the beach and sat together on the docks with their legs dangling above the sea. Though his feet didn't touch the water, it felt like they were being cleansed.

Looking down, he saw that some of the ghosts had begun to depart, so he slowly descended – bad choice of words – feeling like he was being lowered down into a well. When he found he had a better view of the town, he began to soar again, even stretching out his forelegs in an airplane impression. Once more he caught sight of the flying spectres, a huge gathering of them, flocking to a certain spot near the end of town.

Descending further, Randall saw another gathering, this time made of actual living people, including a few police cars. As he got closer, Randall soared down onto the roof of a building. He crouched on his stomach – though he didn't know how discreet he could be with large antlers on his head - and peered over the edge.

People were crowded all around Barnaby's truck, which had

now come to a halt. Many of these people seemed to be trying to get onto Barnaby's truck, but found themselves being held back by some sort of invisible force. Barnaby laughed at them, waving around his cane in victory, right before opening Samantha's cage.

'Look at you all,' said Barnaby into his megaphone, 'All of you wanting to free Santa so he can continue his materialistic regime! Do you know who you remind me of?' He pulled out Samantha, the latter shaking and trying to hold back tears. There she was, the one who caused this whole mess to start with, and here she was, finally getting what she deserved. Not only was she feeling pain, but it was actual physical pain onto her mortal body.

Diane popped into his head again, her scowl along with it. But didn't she want Samantha to suffer? Samantha should just die again, shouldn't she? She was worthless and nasty and nothing. Part of the surplus population, wasn't she?

'This is a young woman who got everything she wanted for Christmas! Piles and piles of disposable gifts bought with money that could be used to feed the poor! She was spoiled as a child and this attitude continued into her adulthood, and this excess led her to her death! I brought her life again out of pity, but when I found out her true nature, I thought that she deserved nothing less than death!' He tightened his grip around Samantha's wrist. From his pocket, he pulled out a knife and hovered it above Samantha's throat. 'And to think, Santa actually wanted her to pull his sleigh! Well, that says a lot about him, doesn't it?'

At this point, the police came in, forcing the people to clear. 'Step away from the girl,' they said. 'Put your hands on your head,' they said. Though Randall was fairly far away from the scene, he knew that Barnaby was reciting a spell. A second later, what looked like a larger version of those annoying ghosts materialized and let loose a large gust of wind, knocking the police backwards.

'You're wasting your time here,' said Barnaby to the now-unconscious policemen, 'Keep my words in mind, tell your children not to expect their usual boatload of presents.'

'Don't listen to him!' In seconds, Randall flew down from his building and stepped onto Barnaby's stage, surprising Barnaby so much he released Samantha. 'I'm one of Santa's reindeer!' yelled Randall, turning attention especially towards the wet-eyed children in the audience. 'I was practicing for tonight when I saw this monster, this…er…naughty, naughty man with a fake Santa, trying to ruin the dreams of children everywhere! He thought it would be a laugh if he used his evil magic to create a fake Santa just because he likes seeing children cry!' He noticed Samantha free of Barnaby's grasp and whispered, 'Run' to her, and she did do just that.

Then he was pretty sure he saw Barnaby mouthing something, which made him float slightly above the stage. The audience all stood wide-eyed and silent.

'So, go back to your homes! Santa Claus will come tonight and deliver your children gifts! There's...agh!' That black spot had appeared again, with claws digging out of it, one of which had grabbed Randall by the ankle. Though Randall struggled and winced, the one consolation he got out of this was that the audience did as he was told.

'There you go, Randall,' sneered Barnaby. 'Samantha told me about you. You're pathetic in Purgatory and you're pathetic on Earth! You know,' he added, grinning as wide as Samantha used to in her reindeer form, 'I might let you go, if you promise to join me.'

'No!' cried Randall. 'You did this for Diane and she rejected it, what makes you think I will?'

'Samantha told me you liked Christmas specials. As much as I don't like the season, I agree with a lot of the messages they give. The Grinch steals all the presents and the people he robbed sing songs of friendship anyway? That wouldn't happen now! I mean, I even saw one Christmas special which suggested limiting children to one present each. Now wouldn't that be something? Less muck cluttering up the house, less demand for disposable trinkets, less pandering...'

Randall broke free from the creature's grasp. 'This is all because you hated your work, isn't it? You went to Toyland when you died, so you must have made stuff for kids, right? I think you said something about a duck one time you were talking to Diane?'

'Indeed,' blurted out Barnaby, 'Those books were merely to pay the bills, and I am to continue writing those as my post-mortem vocation? And nothing else? I wrote poems, essays, and a ridiculous duck is what I'm best known for? And when children read one book, they want more? Forget that! It proves my point; children are greedy and selfish and don't deserve Christmas! Oliver Cromwell had a point, didn't he?'

'Oh brother,' said Randall, before swooping down through Barnaby's body thrice in different directions and then spinning around him in quick circles. When Barnaby fell to the ground, disoriented, Randall flew to the other cages to see if there was a door or lock or anything. Whatever spell Barnaby had used to keep people from his truck didn't work on Randall; something to do with being a spirit, he supposed. 'Randall!' cried Santa, 'Let me out of here!'

'I would if I could,' said Randall as he looked for an opening. 'I don't think there's anything.'

'Let me out of here,' growled Santa, 'I want to talk to Barnaby.'

'You really think you can get them out? They're stuck!' Oh, of course, thought Randall, swiveling around. *Carl and Derek*. Randall had forgotten about them.

'Get away from the cage,' said Derek. 'Not everyone will believe what you said, you know. They'll know we have the real Santa and lose their faith just like we did!'

'Oh god,' said Randall, sighing. 'You people too? Don't you ever shut up about this sort of stuff for once?' At this, they began to whisper something, and the black spot reappeared, a skeletal claw reaching out from it. He flinched, yet he couldn't bring himself to move.

Alice leapt into the scene, stumbling backwards when she saw the crawling spot. She paused for just a second before she whacked Carl over the head with the book, making the spot slow down. Before Derek could make his move, Alice slapped him as well. 'Randall!' she cried. 'I've got the spells!' Carl attempted to snatch the book away, only for Alice to slug him in the chin.

'Read them now!' barked Randall, seeing Barnaby back on his feet. Alice read the spell – as loudly and as quickly as she could before Carl or Derek could make another move - and the reindeers' cages evaporated, with Santa still trapped. 'Quick!' cried Randall as he went to the other reindeer, 'See if you can find a spell for Santa's cage!' Alice looked through the page she was on, while Randall helped Billy out.

'Billy,' said Randall, 'Are you okay?'

'Yeah,' said Billy, 'I'm fine. Just glad I'm not having my butt shocked off.'

'Just run. Fly away and don't come back here. We'll think of a way to get you to Purgatory!'

'I don't want to leave,' said Billy. 'We've got to get Barnaby!'

'But what can we do?' said Randall, looking half at Billy, half at the approaching Barnaby. 'We can't touch him! And he can banish us! Look!' Sure enough, he was reciting a spell, and that black spot began to move again.

'You're really not scared of him, are you?' said Billy. 'Here, you like flying. Let's do what you just did to distract him so she can free Santa.' All the reindeer held each other's hands and took to the sky as if they were the Red Arrows. They flew around for a while as if they were pulling a sleigh, before crashing down to surprise Barnaby…

Randall found himself closest to Barnaby.

Randall hit Barnaby.

He dove down, punched Barnaby in the face and the punch actually connected. Barnaby fell down again, and this time – despite the fact he knew there was an afterlife – he checked to see if Barnaby was dead. His hooves shook and his throat ached. Was his punch really that…and how could…

Barnaby wasn't dead, no. In fact, he stood up almost instantly, snarling at Randall. 'I don't know how you were able to do that,' said Barnaby, 'and I don't care how. As hard as you may have punched me, I still remember my most useful spells, and I can still send you into a pit of no return. All of you!' He pointed at the reindeer, which made all of them growl at him. 'Just think, if you had listened to me, you could have all been reunited with your families by now! Instead, you will neither stay on Earth or on Purgatory!' He yelled the spell at the top of his voice, only to see that black spot fade.

He was fading too.

'What is this?' He and the reindeer turned around to see, on the truck, Samantha reading from the spell book. 'You! You're reversing my resurrection?' Barnaby hobbled over to where Samantha was standing, shaking his fist, only to find himself becoming more and more transparent, even floating off of the ground like he was one of the reindeer.

Though Carl and Derek popped up to try and stop Samantha reading the spell, none other than Billy leapt up and, taking advantage of what Randall displayed, stepped on their fingers. Their screams of pain only served to emphasize the next verse she read.

With the next verse, the now-spectral Barnaby began to glow a fierce orange. His leg disintegrated into nothingness, with his torso still levitating in the air. His arms were the next to crumble, with every tiny segment of him evaporating into nothing.

All that was left was his head and torso. It looked like he was screaming, but no sound emitted from his mouth. There was also no sound when his body was compressed and crushed, reminding Randall of a car he saw being crushed into a cube. With a burst of orange light, Barnaby vanished.

Only to be replaced by something else.

Though Derek and Carl ran away, Randall, Samantha, Alice and the other reindeer watched as the sky turned the same shade of orange Barnaby's spirit did, and a pillar of fire erupted where Barnaby had disappeared. The smell of roasting meat and halitosis filled the air. When that faded away, there stood a fierce red demon, muscular and towering over everyone.

'You had better be using that spell on yourself next,' grunted the demon, its bull horns glimmering with crimson malice, 'then you may have a chance to go back to Purgatory.' Samantha clutched the book tightly, her eyes fixed on the demonic presence before her. 'If you continue that sham of a life,' the demon continued, gnashing his teeth to punctuate his point, 'you join Barnaby.'

Samantha hung her head. 'Yes,' she said forlornly, 'Yes, I was just about to do that.'

The sky resumed its normal colour and in seconds, the demon turned back into no other than Diane. 'Good, just checking.' Randall didn't know whether to sigh or to laugh, so he simply stayed quiet. Alice simply looked surprised.

Samantha, on the other hand, instantly did as she was told. Randall expected her to disintegrate the same way Barnaby did, but rather, all that happened was that there was a blink of light and Samantha was a reindeer again.

'I'm sorry,' was all she said after her transformation.

'I know you are,' said Diane, 'but you will have to do more than apologize to atone for putting us all in this mess.' She turned to the spellbook, still in Samantha's hands, and, with a quick nod of her head, it shot back into Alice's hands. 'As soon as we all get back to Purgatory, that is.'

Samantha told Alice the spells she needed to read, and Alice flicked through the book, plus other pieces of parchment found in the truck, reading the correct spells out loud. One spell made the flying, screeching spectres evaporate into nothingness, and another did the same to Santa's cage. The final spell she was told to read was to restore Diane's power, and as soon as it was spoken, Diane leapt into the air with a light blue glow.

'Yes!' said Diane, raising her arms to embrace her power.

'Wait,' said Alice, 'If you were depowered, how could you turn yourself into a demon like that?'

'Something Paul made,' replied Diane. 'It could only be used once so I just had to wait for the right time.'

'Ho ho ho!' cried Santa as he stretched out. 'I think we truly accomplished something tonight! Randall!'

'Yes?'

'I think I know why your form has gotten more solid. You see, we are more real to the people of Earth the more they believe in us. I and my helpers have tried revealing ourselves on Earth several times in recent years, only to be dismissed as fake or a hallucination. Randall, I am not sure how long this will last, but you appearing to defend me made people believe in me once more, as did Barnaby and his ghosts.' Santa sighed and hung his head, turning away from Randall and towards Diane. 'Diane, I suppose you do have a point. Fear does have its place after all. Without it, our forms would still be gauzy.'

'And,' said Diane, 'It was fear that made Samantha give up, wasn't it, Samantha? Fear of Hell, fear of becoming like Barnaby.'

'Well, yeah,' said Randall, suddenly feeling the urge to join in. 'Christmas isn't just about being happy. I mean, sure there's that, but there's other emotions in there too. Reflecting on the last year and wondering about the next brings all sorts of things; like you feel disappointment, shame and yes, fear. Christmas has presents but it also has embarrassing relatives. There's happy songs, but huge bills. If everything's happy, nothing is.' The only response Randall got from that was everyone simply staring at him. 'Yeah, it's just, this is the part in the Christmas movies where they make a big speech on…oh, never mind.'

'Still, Randall, you did a good job today,' said Santa, his marshmallow tones returning. 'Do you still want to pull my sleigh tonight?' Santa looked to the buildings behind him. 'I think we may need to do some extra houses, too.'

'Yeah,' replied Randall, nodding. 'I'm ready when you are.'

Santa turned to the other reindeer. 'You too?'

They all nodded.

'Samantha,' sighed Santa. 'I trusted you and you betrayed me.' He held her tightly by the wrist. 'I'm afraid you will have to go to the Dark Forest until you are fully cleansed so as to make up for this. I wish there was some other way.'

Samantha said nothing, but her hanging her head and wringing her hands in silence was response enough.

'And speaking of forgiveness.' Once again, he turned to Diane. 'Diane, I am sorry. I have forgotten that I really am in debt to you. I should not have shunned you the way I did. Anything you want in my realm is yours.'

Diane smiled. 'I want your job. I've gotten tired of this spectral journey malarkey; I want to ride around in a sleigh wearing fluffy red gear delivering presents!' Santa groaned. 'Just kidding. See, I can be happy when I want to be! Seriously though, if you want to pay me back, I do think there have to be some changes made to the way you run things in your realm. You could give the more mature stuff a chance for one thing.'

'Very well,' said Santa, stroking his beard like he was a wise wizard. 'I'll take your advice. Alice, prepare the spell to send us back to Purgatory.'

'Okay,' said Alice. 'Randall, I guess this is goodbye.'

'Yeah,' was all Randall could say.

'You said you were more solid now, didn't you?' In seconds, Alice ran up to Randall and gave him a hug, the book still dangling from her fingers. Randall held her as well, and felt truly warm for the first time since he died.

'Goodbye, Alice,' said Randall, once they had released each other. 'I hope you and Lenny have a good life together.'

'Goodbye,' Alice said again, and she began to read out the spell. Randall and the other reindeer. Santa. Diane. All of them grew as gauzy as Barnaby did earlier, only they did not disintegrate the same way he did, rather they just simply popped back to Purgatory. Randall was reminded of the teleporters from *Star Trek*. They were in Santa's workshop, with the warm cold soothing Randall somewhat.

'We're home!' Santa cried before turning his attention to the reindeer. 'Now, we may have been through an ordeal, but you still have a very important job to do, and so do I.'

'Santa.' Diane had come back with them. 'If you need help, may I offer my services?'

Santa nodded, carrying that wise expression seen so often in Christmas cards. 'Of course.'

Diane pulled a list from a shelf. 'Huh. This guy wants a copy of *Amnesia: The Dark Descent*. Knowing you, you weren't going to let him have it. You were going to give him a *Noddy* game or something like that.' Santa blushed. 'Well, you can forget that. Someone wants *Amnesia*, they get *Amnesia*. In fact, I think we should do a wee bit of shopping before tonight, don't you?'

'Yes,' said Santa, 'There's just one thing I have to do first.'

Samantha had come to the workshop too, and found herself being held by Santa again. 'I'm really sorry,' he added.

'Bye, Randall,' said Samantha, 'you know, I think something could have worked between us.' Then she was dragged away to the bogies for who-knows-how-long. Randall almost wanted to go after her, but restrained himself.

Besides, he had to go back to Earth just one more time.

He went back to the little house he had – he flew there to embrace the Purgatory winds – and rested for a while just to clear his mind and get his bearings back. When he felt he had rested enough, he stood on his hind legs and thought about his home. The image he had in his mind of his living room was clearer than any other image he had ever thought of.

In seconds, he was home. His mortal home. The house where his mother lived. Everything was just as it was the last time he was here. There was the Christmas tree, there were the decorations, and there was mum watching TV again. Not just any old TV show either; news about the events Randall had been involved in. They were saying that the ghosts in the sky had vanished, things had calmed down, and of course, that Santa Claus, contrary to popular belief, seemed to actually exist. Randall didn't call to his mother just yet, as he found himself focusing on the news.

He didn't call his mum. His mum called him.

'Randall?' She got off of the sofa and slowly walked towards Randall, giving him a good look. 'Randall!'

'Yeah, mum,' said Randall, scratching the back of his neck. 'It's me. And yes, I am a reindeer now.' He looked at the TV. 'I was there, you know.'

A moment of silence followed between the two before Mum said, 'I know.'

Randall suddenly wondered if there were any paparazzi or something like that where he had his fight with Barnaby and thus had gotten footage of the demonic Diane. If that was true, he didn't know whether to be happy that there existed something that could make Santa even more solid on Earth, or to dread further speculation from the Internet that the Apocalypse was happening.

'I know,' Mum repeated, 'You helped Santa fight against that crooked man with the evil spells. You tried to convince everyone that wasn't the real Santa.'

Randall stood shaking. 'How did you know?'

His mother smiled. 'Your father told me.'

'Dad?' said Randall, half in excitement, half in bewilderment, 'He talked to you?'

'He talked to me a few minutes ago,' replied Mum, having a look around. 'He may even still be here, you know.'

'I think he spoke to me too.'

'He definitely did,' replied Mum, 'He told me he talked to you too. He said he was worried about you.'

'So you know…'

'Yes,' replied Mum. 'He was a reindeer too. He met Santa Claus. The Ghosts from *A Christmas Carol* are real, and he spoke to Diane too.'

'How?'

'Well, he said it's something you can do if you've ascended.'

'Oh…okay.' Randall thought to himself that he shouldn't be surprised given half of the occurrences that had happened to him, so instead he asked if he could just spend a little time with Mum before returning back to Purgatory – just for thirty minutes, Randall said, and Mum, of course, accepted. Away went the news report, and Mum popped in a DVD – a fireplace mood DVD at that. She and her reindeer son just spent half an hour lounging on the sofa staring into the flames.

Randall didn't spend the whole time looking at the pseudo-flames, however. Sometimes he would look askance and saw in the doorway his father. Twice his father had appeared, once as a human and once as a reindeer, looking not too dissimilar to Randall's reindeer form. His ascended father.

Both times he smiled. And it was a real smile.

Epilogue

After Randall returned home, he did more of those training exercises – and without receiving a single trophy either – had a nap, and when the night of Christmas Eve had arrived, he was rested and ready to do the job he was assigned to do.

When he left the house that evening, he saw the sleigh, all polished and shining red. The reindeer were crowded around it; those who had been freed from Barnaby's clutches, and some others too. The ones who had been resurrected, at that. Randall asked about that, and Santa replied they had reversed the spell of their own free will; he had visited the reindeer and their families personally and had explained the situation to them, giving them a choice. Every one of them apparently agreed, though Randall couldn't help but feel a pang of painful curiosity in his gut as he wondered how he got them to agree.

Santa was there. The other reindeer were there. Diane was there too, obviously getting ready for her Christmas Eve job as well, given that she was wearing her robe again and was practicing striking a pose. Randall approached her. 'Hey,' he said, 'Are you all right?'

Diane smiled, and Randall, having gotten used to her rubber-like expressive skull, smiled back. 'I can't complain. I've got my powers back, and since we had all this palaver, I'm pretty sure people are more willing to believe in me like they believe in Santa now.' She chuckled, though it did sound slightly angry. 'Some people who left their shopping until the last minute have decided not to bother, as they think

Santa will provide for them. You've got your work cut out for you tonight.'

'I bet I have,' said Randall, trying to imitate Diane's laugh.

'Maybe,' said Diane, 'Maybe you'll be ascending soon, like, you know, your dad. I really do think you deserve to. That is, unless you want to stay a reindeer until the end of time.'

'Well, I think I should stay here at least a couple more years or so,' said Randall, looking about, 'I mean, Barnaby escaped Hell before, he could do it again. Plus, I really do want to help out around here like you're doing now.'

'Speaking of which,' said Diane, 'I think they're ready to take-off.'

Randall turned around to see Santa waving at him. 'Hurry up, Randall,' he cried, 'we haven't got all night.'

Randall attached himself to the sleigh, giving a thumbs up – or a hoofs up to be technical – and tightened his muscles to ready himself for what would obviously be a Herculean task. Though Randall expected Santa to crack reins or a whip, all Santa did was cry 'Go go go!' and everyone was off.

When he soared off into the purple of Santa's realm - which soon made way for a strangely monochrome sky with black clouds and white clouds – Randall assured himself that flight was one of the new skills he had picked up here that he had truly mastered. Though he was pulling a sleigh rode by a portly man carrying a near-infinite amount of presents, it was one of the lightest things he had ever carried and his legs moved of their own free will – but in a graceful way as opposed to the disjointed way they moved when the ghosts called for him earlier that day.

They soon landed in a neighborhood, and Randall was surprised by how much it resembled a neighborhood from Earth, save the lack of colour. The reindeer landed on a roof of a house, and Santa told them it was by request; the owner wanted to hear the pitter-patter on the roof he thought he had heard as a child. It was the best way for him to sleep easy.

The house didn't have a chimney though, so Santa used the back door. All Purgatory houses that allowed him inside had the usually-locked doors open for him and only him. After Santa delivered the presents for that abode, Randall and the others stayed on the roof for a little while as Santa delivered presents to other houses. Each reindeer, was in fact, fitted with a little coat, which had pockets containing things to help keep them occupied. Little books with puzzles and stories, though ones that wouldn't really challenge anyone older than five. Randall supposed that Diane hadn't gotten around to fixing this little part of the operation yet; maybe he himself would remind Santa sometime in the future.

Santa did a few more houses, and Randall and the others were asked to patter on a few more roofs, and in minutes, they were finished. They moved on to another neighbourhood, one which looked almost identical to the last, with the same song and dance to go with it. Some houses needed a little pitter-patter, the rest of the time Randall did and redid a 5x5 wordsearch.

Randall flew all over Purgatory though, and got a good look at what he had been missing out on from spending so much time in Santa's realm. Away from the samey neighborhoods, there was another built almost entirely with Gothic architecture, making it look like it was comprised of nothing but cathedrals and miniature castles. The sleigh and its workers looked oddly out of place there, Randall thought. Then there was another place where all the houses were shadows, and so were the people from what Randall could see of them.

There was architecture from all sorts of countries and nations, buildings made of mud, stone and various other materials, other places covered with snow, even something that looked like an Escher painting. Randall remembered when he looked out of the window while on a train and thought about going for 'a tramp in some of the places he passed on a sunny day. Maybe one day he'd get to see some of these places in more detail.

When the Purgatory rounds were complete, Randall and all the other reindeer were asked to close their eyes and picture a specific place on Earth, one close to where today's troubles had started. Soon, they materialized onto Earth and had a surprisingly quick delivery round too. Randall had done everything he needed to here, so he simply just waited for Santa to finish his deliveries and had a constant look around for any magic-users or paparazzi.

They flew around the city, and another, and another, the whole trip around the world becoming a blur. Randall was back at the workshop before he knew it. Maybe it was because Earth paled in comparison to what he saw in Purgatory. Something told him it wouldn't be the last time he would see those places, and it wouldn't be while delivering either.

When the rounds were complete, the tradition was that the

reindeer received their own gifts for a job well done. Billy got a Kindle because he read so much on his breaks. That one over there received a portable console. Randall was never one to ask for much, so he received less in comparison, but what he did receive still meant a lot.

A photo of his mother and father, one he could hang in his little home among the little winter scenes, and a little scrapbook of him and Alice. Things from his old home he didn't take with him. Also a copy of *A Christmas Carol*, the original Dickens book, signed by Diane.

The next evening, Santa threw his annual party to celebrate their annual accomplishments. The workshop was cleared of its tables and tools for the reindeer and elves to have a dance, and in the entertainment center, the movies were playing as usual, this time with a table of refreshments nearby.

It was also the first party Diane was invited to. She arrived at about the same time Randall did, bringing along what Randall learned was the latest Ghost of Christmas Past – Diane said his name was Marcus and while he hadn't ascended, 'he was on the right path'. She had brought other things as well, but had brought them earlier that day. The party would still have the usual eggnog and fizzy pop, but there would also be plenty of Carling and Guinness available too. Randall walked upstairs to the entertainment centre to see the elves watching not a Christmas movie, but rather jumping and laughing at a slasher flick.

'Randall!' said Santa as he came up the stairs. 'Thank you for pulling my sleigh.'

'Well, thanks for the present,' said Randall. 'Much appreciated.'

'You're more than welcome. Now, why don't we have a couple of beers and a film?'

Randall, Santa and Diane all grabbed a Carling and joined the elves in watching the slasher. Santa had feared such a movie would corrupt his helpers' minds, but laughed along with them at the terrible effects and apathetic acting. This was followed by the first couple of *Breaking Bad* episodes, which Santa responded to by saying, 'I want more.'

After a while of being a couch potato, Randall went downstairs to find several reindeer and elves on the pseudo-dance floor. One female reindeer – not Samantha – instantly pulled him off the stairs and danced with him, begging Randall to copy her moves. They were later joined by Santa and Diane and despite some uncertain glances from the other dancers, Diane and Santa danced together, twirling each other around and synchronizing their movements.

They danced the night away, and soon the party was over, with nobody left in the workshop except for Diane, Santa, and even Randall, for that female reindeer had left with someone else.

'Well,' said Randall, 'You two seemed to be enjoying yourselves.'

'Oh yeah,' said Diane, 'Just like old times.'

'No,' said Santa, 'It felt…new. I should try new things more often.'

About the Author

Gareth Barsby is a graduate of the University of Chester, where he studied Creative Writing and Journalism, but for most of his life, he has used writing to explore weird new worlds. He has a blog where he puts up his written work - myweirdwriting.wordpress.com has self-published three books - THE WEREWOLF ASYLUM, BARKING BENJAMIN and MR. MOVIE-MAKER – and has submitted short stories to several publications.

Printed in Great Britain
by Amazon